ADRYEL

JON TRUMAN

Dedicated to
Julie and Jennifer

Thanks to
Linda Denison Sass
L.M. Patience

PROLOGUE

"My name is Adryel. I am an angel. A guardian angel to be exact. My mission is to serve the elect. That is, to serve those who now believe in Christ and those who, in time, will believe…"

"WHY ARE YOU DOING THIS?" Her name was Paige. She was seventeen. Kidnappers had seized her, her father, and mother along with several others. They took them to an abandoned cabin deep in the woods of North Georgia. Soon after, they dragged them into a weathered dull gray barn fifty yards from the cabin. They duck-taped her to a chair in the upstairs hay loft__.

"Usually, we are assigned to watch over and protect an individual. I say 'usually' because my last assignment, which I will soon share with you, was an *unusual* one. I was called to keep a close watch over *two* families. Both were about to face the worst time of their lives.

"I'm speaking of Jesse Striker, his wife Melissa and their ten year old daughter, Abigail, and their best friends, Billy Whitecloud, his wife, Woya, their eleven year old daughter Chloe and their nine year old son, Nathan…"

"WHAT ARE YOU GOING TO DO?" One of her kid-nappers stood facing her in his biker rags, a gas can in his hand__.

"Before I share what they endured and how at times, I interceded on their behalf, allow me to clear up some misconceptions about us. Contrary to what many believe, we *do* have bodies. They are just not as you envision them. Should I appear on earth, which I have on several occasions, I do so invisibly or in a body that would appear just like yours. In heaven though, I have no need of a physical body. Our essential nature is that of a spirit, or a created being without a physical body.

"But again, I do have a body, a *spiritual* body that can be seen and touched. In that sense, our bodies are quite similar to the souls of humans who are now in heaven. Of course, human souls will receive a new, imperishable body that is in substance, physical, shortly after Christ returns to earth. We will remain as we now are…"

She could hear her father's voice as it floated up to the loft. They had tied him to a beam below. He was pleading with someone. "Just let us go. I can get you money. A lot of money. And none of us will say a thing. Please…"

There was a loud popping sound, like—like gun fire.

"DAD!" she screamed. But he didn't respond.

*As the kidnapper slowly shuffled toward her, she could
hear the others screaming— her mother, Olivia, her aunt
Andrea and her twelve year old cousin Madison__.*

"And, by the way, if you were thinking we have
wings, you would be wrong. We don't. We move about
by thought. As for our size, in terms of your earthly mea-
surements, I am seven feet-five-inches tall. That's about
average here. But regardless of my or any angel's size, each
of us has, to varying degrees, *nearly* unlimited power. Not
total power, mind you. Only the Father, Son, and Holy
Spirit have that. But, each of us has the power to do what
on earth you would call, miraculous. Such power is one
of the necessary gifts we are given in order to do what we
are often called on to do.

"Another point of clarification: following the death
of a loved one, some have been comforted by the unexpected appearance of that loved one, believing it to really
be them. That certainly is possible. Those who have
gone on to heaven *can* indeed appear on earth. Case in
point, Moses and Elijah. They appeared at the Mount of
Transfiguration. But such appearances of loved ones who
have passed on are the exceptions, not the rule.

"Usually, what one is seeing is their angel, for should
we make an appearance, we would look just like the
ones we serve. Remember Peter? When miraculously
freed from prison, he knocked on the door of those who

were praying for him. When told it was Peter, they didn't believe it. Instead, one said, "It is his angel…"

"NO…PLEASE…NO…" she screamed as her kidnapper poured gasoline around her chair, and then—on her. It drenched her hair, her clothing and burned her eyes. She whimpered and squinted as he backed toward the ladder, pouring a trail of gas before descending to the dirt floor below. He doused the others and then poured a path to the open barn door.

"Ready?" he said. And after others surrounded the outside of the barn, splashing gas on the weathered, dried boards, he struck a match and tossed it on the dirt floor. There was a loud WHOOSH, and the flames raced inside, engulfing those below. They charged up the ladder, shimmering toward her and enveloping her. She disappeared in the flames, thrashing wildly, screaming her last scream until mercifully—she slumped forward.

"That brings me to the story I want to share with you. To fully comprehend it, it's best that you understand what led up to it."

CHAPTER 1

It all began twelve years ago. Less than two hours after Jesse Striker and Jenny Whitecloud had said their wedding vows, Jenny was murdered. Months passed and the police had made no progress. Frustrated, Jesse and Jenny's brother, Billy, a private investigator, decided to find Jenny's murderer.

In the months that followed, they captured Beau Haggart, aka Ironman. A jury of his peers convicted him of first degree murder and sentenced him to life without parole at Georgia State Prison.

Unfortunately for Jesse, the hoped-for closure never materialized. Instead, in the days and months that followed, he experienced a hellish, recurring nightmare that forced him to relive that day again and again. And it was always the same.

The evening wedding is over, and Jesse is in the basement of the Cherokee Lutheran Church enjoying the reception. All the wedding party is present except Jenny Whitecloud, his new bride. Clad in her wedding gown, she has left her guests to get a gift for her father that is locked in Jesse's car.

Jesse is talking with a guest when, in mid-sentence, he hears the guttural, rumbling of many motorcycles.

Only—this is different. The sound is slow, deep, and sinister. When finally it fades, it is replaced by a more frightening sound.

A scream.

It's Jenny.

Her voice sounds like it's coming from deep within the bowels of an ancient stone well. Jesse reacts instantly. He bounds up the basement steps two at a time, slams through the front doors of the church onto the porch. Only—he is floating in slow motion, like—a man running on the moon.

Jenny screams again, "JEEEESSSSSEEEEEE!"

Her voice is thick, like molasses flowing from a bottle. At the sound of it, Jesse's head gradually rotates ninety degrees in Jenny's direction. His eyes slowly widen and his heart stops when he sees her.

Two men on either side of her hold her arms while a biker in black leather grasps her face in a vice-grip and attempts to kiss her.

Like a man running in waist-deep water, Jesse glides off the porch. "JENNNNEEEEE," he yells.

In perfect synchronization, the eyes of a dozen or more bikers turn in his direction as he bursts through them in slow-motion, knocking two of them to the ground.

He fights his way to the man in black, but—two men grab him from behind. The man in black steps up to him and punches him again and again.

Another sound pierces the air.

Sirens.

Many of them, sounding like CD's playing in reverse.

The men drop Jesse and he slumps to the ground. Though groggy, he hears a voice. It's the man in the black. Like the sound of one possessed by demons, he yells, "LEEETSSSSMOOOVEEEIIITT."

It echoes as the bikers float toward their Harleys and, one by one, drift down the driveway.

Then—Jesse hears another voice.

"JEEESSSSSEEEE."

It's Jenny. Once again, she screams as she glides toward Jesse and kneels by his side.

Jesse turns and sees the man in black. He just reaches the road when suddenly he spins his bike around and twists the throttle wide open. Smoke plumes from around the back tire as it spins and burns. The cycle lurches forward, its front tire rises in the air, and then—falls.

The man in black now stands, straddling his Harley. In slow-motion, he reaches in his boot, pulls out something black, and points it in Jesse's direction.

Jesse hears a muffled explosion and an exaggerated thudding sound as a bullet slams into the waist of Jenny's wedding dress. A flower of red blooms on white satin, and Jesse screams—"NOOOOOOOOOOO!"

And then Jesse jerks awake. He springs into a sitting position, gasps, then—lays his head back on the damp pillow and shivers.

CHAPTER 2

Devastated and without faith to cope, Jesse could not be consoled. It wasn't until something remarkable happened. Several months later, Jenny's angel appeared to him. At first, he didn't know what to think. But, hoping that maybe Jenny was somehow alive, he asked Billy to accompany him to church where he could do something he had never done before—pray.

Now, as a committed believer, he often recalls the moment of his conversion. It was 8:40 p.m. He had met his brother-in-law, Billy Whitecloud, outside the Cherokee Lutheran Church.

"You okay?" Billy asked.

"Yeah…yeah…I'm okay. Shall we?" Jesse opened the church door and Billy stepped inside. As Jesse closed it behind him, he said, "Would you mind sitting in the back while I go up front and pray?"

Billy simply nodded and slipped into a back pew while Jesse slowly walked down the green carpeted aisle toward the front. The thought that God would not help him, and that he would leave as lost as he now was, crept into his mind and all of a sudden, he felt like a dead man walking.

Jesse stopped near the second pew on his left, and froze. His eyes slowly rose to the huge cross centered on the wall, high above the altar, then to the altar itself, and the three-foot crucifix that sat there, an altar candle on either side.

Jesse took a deep breath, slipped into the pew and sat. He took out the cross Jenny's father had given her on their wedding day. Engraved on the back were the words "i-tsu-la i-go-hi-dv", Cherokee for "Together Forever." He clutched it tightly in the sweaty palm of his right hand—and prayed.

"God, I've never talked to you before. You know that. I don't even know if you're there or…if you are, whether you'd listen to a guy like me. I certainly don't deserve it. But God…oh God…I need you so bad."

Jesse's eyes glazed and a tear broke free and ran down his cheek. He wiped it away with the knuckle of his left index finger, and opening the palm of his right hand, he stared at Jenny's cross.

All of a sudden, it seemed to move.

Jesse's heart skipped a beat as he blinked away the tears so he could see better. Sure enough, ever so slowly, it was rising out of his hand and floating up—up—until it hung suspended in mid-air before him.

Had Jesse been granted the privilege given only a few, he would have seen Jenny's angel standing before him, the cross in her hand.

And then, something else happened, something that caused his eyes to open even wider and his heart, which had skipped a moment earlier, to begin to race and pound. The cross—

Slowly, it was turning, turning until the words—"Together Forever"—were facing him.

"Jenny?"

That's when something else totally unexpected happened. Right after the cross descended back into his palm, he caught a whiff of lilac. Jenny's perfume.

"Jenny…is it you?" Jesse then remembered that it wasn't really Jenny, but her angel. "Please," he said. "Would you give Jenny a message? Tell her I love her, and that I miss her so much." Jesse's voice broke and the tears of joy flowed as they had never flowed before.

"Thank you, Jesus…thank you, Jesus!" Jesse repeated those three words over and over again. And then, like the sun breaking through the clouds, he felt a peace and warmth. It was as if Jenny were hugging him. The truth is, though he could not see it, her angel was. Nor could he see her when she moved her lips to within an inch of his ear and whispered the first Cherokee words Jenny had taught him, the words for "I love you"— A-ya-tsi-ni-hi.

CHAPTER 3

Twelve years later.

By the grace of God, the nightmares gradually tapered off and then ended abruptly. Oddly, it happened on the one year anniversary of Jenny's murder.

From that point forward, things began to change. Jesse and Jenny's maid of honor and best friend, Melissa, began to date. A year later, two years after the tragic murder of Jesse's first love, they were married. Ten months flew by and Abigail was born. In all, twelve years had passed since Jenny's death.

Jesse was now thirty-seven. Professionally, he had become a successful writer of Christian suspense novels. Four of the six had edged their way on the *New York Times* best seller list.

Beside that, and his marriage, little else had changed. He still lived in the same log cabin in Wears Valley, Tennessee. Physically, he still had a middle-weight version of a Schwarzenegger build, though admittedly, he had added five pounds. Fortunately, most of it was muscle, thanks to his five-day workout at the "Y."

He still had a black belt in Tae Kwon Do, but since his conversion, he was loath to use his skill. He vowed to do so only if absolutely necessary. The idea of hurting another had become repugnant to him.

As for Melissa, little had changed. At five-foot-six, she was still three inches shorter than Jesse, still had those beautiful light blue eyes, flawless skin and striking blond hair. She still carried a few extra, well-proportioned pounds. And she was still pleasantly out-spoken, determined, and tenacious. When she made up her mind, changing it was next to impossible. Not a good trait when wrong, but critically important when you're right. And in Jesse's estimation, she was right more times than wrong.

One other thing about Melissa, her love for her circle of college friends: Jesse, Billy, and yes—even to this day—Jenny, was stronger than ever. Although Jenny was no longer with them physically, she was with them in spirit. She was alive and well. Just in a far better place.

The birth of her and Jesse's daughter, Abigail, along with Billy's wife Woya, and their children, Chloe and Nathan—only expanded Melissa's circle of friends.

When she first met Woya, she asked what her name meant.

"It's Cherokee for Dove," Woya said.

"Really?" Melissa paused. "Thanks for sharing that. Wado."

Woya raised her eyebrows in surprise. "You know Cherokee?"

"Uhh…I know the words for 'Thank you.' Jenny taught me. But, I'm afraid that's about it."

"Maybe I'll teach you some more."

"I'd like that."

Woya smiled, wrapped her arms around Melissa. She gave her a warm hug, pulled back, and said, "Wado."

From that day forward Melissa and Woya became best friends. Both looked forward to their every Sunday gathering at Billy and Woya's Gatlinburg A-frame bungalow or Jesse and Melissa's Wears Valley cabin.

In the early years following Jenny's murder, the name Ironman occasionally surfaced. But, as time gently washed away the sharp edges of pain, his name ceased to come up. It was all in the past, for Ironman was safely locked away in Georgia State prison serving a sentence of life without parole.

CHAPTER 4

Thursday.

Georgia State Prison was located in one of those "blink-and-you'll-miss-it" towns—Reidsville, Georgia, population, 2,500. Securely housed behind two, twenty-foot high, chain-link fences topped with razor wire, were some of Georgia's worst felons. Fifty-five hundred at last count.

Much like Arrendale, Augusta, Hays, and Metro State, Georgia State was a level VI, maximum security prison. It was the home of convicted felons with a history of violence in prison and those who had been convicted of heinous crimes.

Fifty-four year old warden, Roland Cartwright, sat behind his scarred oak desk in his fourteen-by-fourteen foot office. To make up for the lack of light that barely filtered in through the one barred window, a double fluorescent buzzed overhead.

Besides a scuffed up, ink-stained desk blotter, the only thing on the warden's desk was a ten-year-old picture of himself (weighing forty pounds less), his wife, Olivia, his then seven-year old daughter Paige, and his younger brother—now thirty-five year old, Seth.

A former small town police captain and now warden of Georgia State Prison, Roland Cartwright was a bit of a paradox. He professed to be a Christian and strongly encouraged new inmates to attend Sunday services. Never mind that he'd never quite acquired the habit.

The truth is, if he had any genuine faith, it hadn't advanced beyond the "Jesus Loves Me, This I Know" stage.

Sitting across from him in one of two primitive oak desk chairs was head guard, Jimmy Sanders. Having gone over the routine for the morning, Cartwright gave him one last assignment. "Get me Beau Haggart. His grandma just died. I suspect he might want to attend her funeral."

"You think he deserves to go?"

"No. But…I hate to think how much trouble he'll cause us if we don't let him. Just…get him in here."

Five minutes later, shackled hand and foot, Beau Haggart, alias Ironman, shuffled into the warden's office in his prison-issued orange jumpsuit. Sanders stood behind him. "Have a seat, Haggart," the warden said, nodding toward the door for Sanders to leave.

Cartwright couldn't help but notice that Haggart hadn't changed all that much since his incarceration twelve years ago. According to his chart, which lay in front of him, Haggart still weighed 185 pounds, still stood at an even six foot, and still had those intimidating "Get-out-of-my-face" Jack Nicholson eyes.

He still had a pocked face and that hideous scar that cut from his right temple, sliced over his cheekbone, and zigzagged downward across his lips to his chin. One could only imagine what had caused that.

Haggart's arms were still black with tattoos, including the ominous horned head of the devil indelibly inked onto his right shoulder.

"Haggart, I'm afraid I've got some bad news."

"What's new?"

Cartwright ignored the sarcasm. "I'm afraid your grandmother has passed."

Ironman's spine stiffened and his head slowly rose in a vain "nothing-bothers-me" pose. It might have worked had it not been for the glaze that suddenly appeared in his eyes.

"When?"

"Yesterday."

"When's the funeral?"

"Day after tomorrow. Saturday."

There was a brief pause. "I wanna' go."

Warden Cartwright gave Ironman his best look of concern, "It can be arranged."

Reluctantly, Beau Haggart said, "Thanks."

"You want me to say a prayer?" the Warden said, hoping Haggart would say 'No.' Cartwright let out an inaudible sigh of relief when Ironman slowly shook his head from side to side.

Saturday.

Born of a drug dependant prostitute and one of her Johns, a now discredited politician, Beau Haggart had been raised by his maternal grandmother. Her name was Hazel Phillips. His name, Haggart, was made up.

Had it not been for his grandmother, Beau would have never experienced what love is. But Hazel loved Beau. And Beau loved her in return. He took care of her during the waning years of her life, when she was blind and confined to a wheel chair.

Following his capture and incarceration, he was daily haunted by the thought that he would never see her again. And the anger he had felt toward Billy Whitecloud and Jesse Striker smoldered within him. The thought of getting even never left him.

That his grandmother had now died only fanned that hatred as he bounced along in the prison van bound for Macon and the George Moran Funeral Home. Throughout the journey, he fumed as he alone sat in the back of the van, shackled hand and foot.

He had asked the warden to let him wear his one suit, but—he was denied. At least, once inside the funeral home, he would be un-shackled. But he'd still be wearing his prison-issued orange jumpsuit with DEPARTMENT OF CORRECTIONS printed on the back. He hated the warden for that, but not as much as he detested

Whitecloud and Striker. They were the reason he was in prison, not the Warden.

Following a brief eulogy and banal message from some "whoever-they-could-find" retired pastor, Beau stepped up to the casket and leaned way forward, his lips inches from his grandmother's ears. Tears that he had succeeded in holding back, now burst forth as he whispered his last words to the one person he had loved more than life itself, "I'll make em' pay, Grandma!"

Following the graveside service, the ride back to Georgia State Prison, and supper in the cafeteria, Beau got in line to call Ricardo Sanchez. He was second-in-command of Beau's motorcycle gang, the Georgia Ex-Cons.

Beau had selected him to "hold-the-fort," while he was incarcerated. The reason was, next to Beau, Sanchez was the meanest of the Ex-Cons. Most thought he had no conscience whatsoever. Evidence suggested that might not be true. Even so, were he attacked, he would do whatever it took to win. If that meant jamming his fingers into another's eyes and blinding him, so be it. If it meant smashing ones nose into their brain insuring they would never again see the light of day, he wouldn't give it a second thought. That he had been an enforcer for the now deceased Mexican drug lord, Pablo Carballo, only added to his credits.

As the convict before him finished his call, Beau picked up the wall phone and dialed Sanchez's number. He answered on the third ring.

"Sanchez."

"Hey. It's me. Ironman. I want you to come see me next Saturday. Visiting hours are 10 to noon and 1 to 3:00. Come around 10:00."

"Any particular reason?"

"Oh…you bet." Knowing the calls were monitored, Beau was not about to share the real reason why.

"Well, let's just say…I miss you, buddy. I need a little company."

"Yeah. Right." Sanchez chuckled. "I'll be there."

"Bring Snake."

"Will do," Sanchez said before hanging up.

CHAPTER 5

A week later.

Saturday, 8:00 a.m.

Early June.

Sanchez stood in front of one of Macon's three Hardees' restaurants. His Harley Fat Boy beside him was still cooling as he impatiently glanced at his watch and frowned. Fortunately, he wouldn't have to wait long. He could hear the ever increasing rumbling of another Harley. It was Snake. It had to be.

Snake, of course, was not his real name. That was his biker name, one given him by Ironman. When asked why, Ironman had said, "Because you're as skinny as a snake and twice as mean."

And he was. Next to Ironman and Sanchez, Snake ranked third when it came to downright meanness.

"Where in the h___ you been," Sanchez said as Snake pulled his Harley Night Rod beside Sanchez's cycle.

"D___, what am I…a minute late? Gee. You need to pop a pill, man."

Snake had modified his Harley to get, what he called, "maximum thunder." You'd swear you could hear him coming a mile away.

"You ought to tune that sucker down."

"Why would I want to do that?" Snake said as he shut off his Harley.

It seemed to Sanchez that Snake was yelling, which he was. You can only take Harley-enhanced decibel overload so long.

As both entered Hardees and strutted up to the counter, all eyes surreptitiously took them in, and—for good reason. Both were dressed to kill, though not in the positive sense of the word. They were decked out in traditional Georgia Ex-Con black leather from head to toe. Both wore do-rags and sported innumerable tattoos. The Ex-Con logo on the back of their jackets didn't help.

Thirty minutes and two orders of buttermilk fried chicken smothered in sausage gravy, hash browns, eggs, and "made-from-scratch" biscuits later—they fired up their Harleys and roared onto Highway 16 south. Reidsville, Georgia State Prison, and Ironman, were 117 miles away.

A little over an hour and a half later, Sanchez and Snake pulled outside the main entrance to Georgia's maximum security prison.

"Man, I hate being here. Brings back too many bad memories," Snake said.

"Well, at least, we won't have to stay."

As they rode their cycles through the gate and pulled up to the guard house, two guards greeted them with less than enthusiastic stares. Several minutes and numerous clanking iron doors later, they found themselves in the visitors' room.

"Do you see Ironman?" Sanchez asked.

Scanning the forty or more tables and at least twice as many visitors—wives, children, mothers and a few fathers—they didn't see Ironman anywhere.

They sat at an empty table for four and waited. Just then, an interior door opened and in came three more prisoners dressed in orange jumpsuits. One of them was Ironman. He walked up to the table, pulled out a chair, and sat.

"Good to see you, man," Snake said.

"Yeah. You too."

"So...how have they been treating you?" Sanchez asked.

"How do you think?"

A moment of silence followed. Sanchez broke it when he said, "Why did you want to see us? Sounded like something more than you just wanting to look at our pretty faces."

"I want some payback. I want you guys to make that injun and Striker guy wish they'd never been born."

"What do you have in mind?"

"Why don't you try this for starters...?"

* * *

Although no one could see him, Adryel stood no more than five feet away. He was leaning back on a nearby

22

grey cinderblock wall, his muscular arms folded. His eyes were intently locked on Ironman, Sanchez, and Snake.

He could tell from their conversation and from his heightened senses that they were planning something bad. He didn't know exactly what it was, for unlike the Father, Son, and Holy Spirit, neither he nor any angel could read minds. That said, given his assignment to watch over the Whiteclouds and the Strikers, he knew that whatever Ironman had planned would be directed at them.

At the close of the visiting hour, Sanchez and Snake rose to leave while Ironman and thirty or more cons lined up to return to their cells. Adryel's eyes followed Ironman as he was leaving. And then—he disappeared.

CHAPTER 6

Wednesday.

8:30 a.m.

Knoxville's FBI Bureau Chief, Larry Harrelson, pressed the speed dial button on his cell phone. Billy answered on the third ring. "Whitecloud Investigations. This is Billy. How can I help you?"

"What makes you think I want your help?"

"Seriously? Why else would you call?"

"Because…we're good friends?"

"Like I said, why else would you call?"

"Well, the truth is, I've got a little favor to ask of you."

"And…what might that be, Agent Harrelson?"

"How formal, Mr. Whitecloud. The fact is, I need you to do something for me. We have a new agent arriving at McGhee Tyson at 10:00 a.m. Friday. I'm tied up, and so are my agents. You mind meeting her at the airport and bringing her here?"

"Not at all. Only one problem. I'm tied up too. But, tell you what I'll do. I'll give Jesse a call. If he can't do it, I'll find someone."

"Great. I appreciate it!"

"Question. How will she know who is meeting her?"

"I told her we'd have someone holding an FBI sign."

"That oughta' work."

"Thanks, my friend. You're the best."

"You say that to all your gophers."

"Yeah. I guess I do." Harrelson hung up.

*   *   *

Billy called Jesse.

"Striker."

"Jesse. This is Billy. I wonder if you can do something for me. Check that. I wonder if you can do something for Harrelson."

"Sure. What is it?"

"He needs someone to drop by McGhee Tyson to pick up a new agent that's been transferred to the Knoxville office."

"And why can't you or one of Harrelson's agents do this?"

"They're busy. Me too."

"And, I'm not?"

"You're an author for Pete's sake. You're never busy."

"You trying to butter me up or something?"

Jesse's mind momentarily flitted back to when he and Billy were college roommates at the University of Tennessee in Knoxville. As a quiet spoken, six-foot-three, full-blooded Cherokee who rarely smiled—to those who didn't know him, he was intimidating.

"You know," Jesse said, "you used to be a quiet sort of guy, one who'd scare people. And now you're a comedian?"

"People change."

"That they do. So…how am I going to recognize her?"

"That's a piece of cake. Just look for a gorgeous five-foot-ten redhead with creamy white skin and heavenly light blue eyes."

"Really?"

"No. According to Harrelson, she's actually a five-foot-seven Japanese American. But Harrelson says, she *is* gorgeous."

"Does she have a name?"

"Does she have a name? Of course, she has a name."

"And pray tell, what might her name be?

"Masumi. Masumi Takara."

"And how is Ms. Takara supposed to recognize me?"

"That's easy. I suggested that Harrelson tell her to look for a short, homely guy in his late thirties who'd be holding up a sign that said FBI."

"You know, Whitecloud, I've gotta' hand it to you. You sure know how to get a guy to do something for you. But, being the good guy I am, I'll do it. What time did you say?"

"10:00 a.m. Friday."

"I'm on it."

Jesse hung up.

CHAPTER 7

Thursday evening

6:15 p.m.

As was their custom, Jesse and Melissa were sitting in front of the TV, eating supper, and watching FOX News. For reasons unknown, Jesse had acquired the habit of sitting on the floor before the coffee table. Melissa sat in a chair. Blond haired, blue eyed Abigail, or Abby as she preferred to be called, was the only one who actually sat at the kitchen table. The reason was—she wasn't interested in the news. What ten-year old is? Besides, she could eat and text her friends.

"Great meal, hon."

"Of course."

And it was. Meatloaf, mashed potatoes with brown gravy, buttermilk biscuits, and green beans flavored with bacon grease."

As a flood of commercials followed the news, Jesse said to Melissa, "Got a call from Billy yesterday. He asked me to do a favor for Harrelson."

"The FBI agent?"

"Yep."

"What did he ask you to do?"

"Pick up a new agent at the airport. Some Japanese American beauty who loves authors."

Melissa squinted at Jesse, her face masked in faux concern.

Jesse grinned and rose to take his plate to the kitchen. He rinsed it and put it in the sink. Then, turning to Abigail, he said, "Don't forget the dishes."

"Why do I have to always do the dishes?"

"Well...because I said...do the dishes?" Smiling, Jesse slipped over to Abby and kissed her on the head. "Okay Ab?"

"It's Abby, not...Ab."

"Sorry. I forgot."

"And by the way, all you have to do is stick em' in the dishwasher. Difficult, I know, but doable."

Jesse then turned and headed for his office. Once there, he did what he always did—check his e-mails, peruse Facebook, then read a few chapters of a novel by one of his favorite authors.

By 9:30, Abigail was in bed. Like clockwork, Jesse joined Melissa in the family room. They watched a news program, then one of their favorite TV series. They went to bed around midnight. It was always the same. Except for—this Thursday evening—

2:30 a.m.

As they lay in bed, asleep, moonlight filtering in through the muntins of the window cast elongated square patches of light on the bedspread.

Suddenly—

They were awakened by a loud sound. It was guttural. Rumbling. So loud, the bedroom windows rattled. Jesse jerked awake and sat up. *What the...?*

When the fog of sleep lifted, both he and Melissa knew what it was. Motorcycles. Harleys. Lots of them. Clearly, they were on the driveway.

"Daddy?"

It was Abby. She had run into their bedroom. "What is that?"

"Motorcycles. Don't worry. Just stay here with Mom." Abby jumped into her parents' bed and pulled the covers up to her chin.

Melissa scooted back to the headboard. She clutched the bed sheet tightly and drew it to her chest, while Jesse threw off the covers and sat on the edge of the bed. He pulled open the night stand drawer and withdrew his Keltec 32. He rose, stepped up to the closet, and removed a gun clip he had hidden there. For safety reasons, he had kept both his gun and clip separate ever since the day Abigail was born.

That he even owned a gun was something he thought he'd never do. Why would he need it? He had a black belt in Tae Kwon Do. There was just one problem. Make that two.

For one thing, Billy had said, "What are you going to do if they pull a gun? Huh? To make his point, Billy thrust his open palm into Jesse's chest, quickly yanked his gun from his holster, and pointed it at Jesse. "By the time you get your balance back, I've shot you.

"Jesse, your martial arts are good only in close quarters. You know that. Besides," he added, "even if you weren't a black belt, by the time the police arrive, if someone's determined to 'off' you, it'll be 'lights out.' Police are *reactive*, not *proactive*. They don't arrive before a crime is committed; they arrive after. That's a little late if someone's determined to put the 'big sleep' on you."

So Jesse purchased a gun. He also got his carrying permit. He now stood, and slipped through the bedroom door into the hall.

With gun in hand, he padded toward the back door. As he stepped on the porch, the staccato rumbling of numerous Harleys began to fade. By the time he reached the end of the porch and stepped on the driveway, he could see the taillights of several Harleys as they thundered away.

CHAPTER 8

Thursday evening

3:45 a.m.

"Mommy…Daddy…what's all that noise?"

It was Nathan. He had run into his parents' bedroom. Chloe was close behind.

Having stayed up too late, Billy and Woya were fast asleep. Neither heard what had awakened Nathan and Chloe. Now, as the cobwebs of their mind began to clear, they knew what it was. Motorcycles. And then, there was the smashing, tinkling sound of breaking glass.

Billy jumped out of bed. "STAY HERE," he shouted as he charged into the living room and ran up to the picture window. It was shattered. Through the broken shards, he could see the taillights of several motorcycles, descending his driveway for Ski Mountain Road.

He turned, took three steps, and stubbed his toe on— on what?

Billy knelt. Unable to see what it was in the dark, he ran his hand on the carpet and then—he knew. It was a brickbat.

To cover the hole, Billy walked to the back porch and to the nearby well house. It was just a few feet from the steps. He grabbed a piece of one inch Styrofoam left over from insulating the door. With that, and some duct tape, he sealed the hole in the window. When he returned to the bedroom, Nathan and Chloe were snuggled up to Woya.

"Well, somebody has thrown a brickbat through our window."

"I'm scared, Daddy," Nathan said.

"It's okay. They're gone."

"Who did that?" Chloe asked.

"I don't know, hon," he said as he cast a knowing look at Woya. They both knew who had done this. Who it had to be. Ironman's thugs.

"Can we sleep with you?" Nathan asked.

"Sure," Billy said. And trying to instill an element of calm, he added, "But you guys better move over a bit and make some room for me or…I'll squish you."

* * *

Friday morning.

8:00 a.m.

The first thing Friday morning, Billy called Jesse. "You awake?"

"Sure. What's up?"

"Anything strange happen at your home last night?"

"Oh yeah. We were assaulted by motorcycles. Ironman's, of course. How about you?"

"Same. They threw a brickbat through our window. What did they do to you guys?"

"Good question. They were in our driveway and, I saw them leave. I didn't think to check to see what, if anything, they had done. Hold on."

Jesse stepped on the back porch and walked to the drive way. That's when he saw the tires of his Cobalt had been slit. "You still there," he said to Billy.

"Yeah."

"They cut my tires. Just a minute."

Jesse walked to the other side of his car and looked down at the other tires, and frowning, he said, "All four."

"Okay. Listen, I've gotta go. But, we need to talk about what to do next. I'll give you a call later."

Billy hung up and Jesse returned to the kitchen where Melissa was frying eggs. He gave her a hug as Abigail pulled out a chair and sat.

"Good morning, Miss Abby."

"Morning, Dad."

Jesse sat. "I don't have much time," he said as Melissa set a plate of bacon and eggs before him. "Gotta' pick up the new agent."

"The beautiful one who loves authors?"

"Yeah. That one. There's only one problem. The tires on the Cobalt have been slit."

"You're kidding!"

"I wish I were." Without mentioning their name, Jesse then shared what Ironman's gang had done to the Whiteclouds.

"So—I need to borrow you car. Is that okay?"

"Fortunately, it is. I have no plans to go anywhere."

"Great. You're the best."

"Everyone says that."

CHAPTER 9

Friday morning.

McGhee Tyson Airport

Jesse arrived at McGhee Tyson at 9:15 and parked. Ten minutes later, he was standing among fifty or more who were awaiting the arrival of friends or family to walk down the ramp. Another five minutes passed, and passengers began to appear, but no—*what's-her-name? Masumi something.*

There was a lull in the arrival of passengers and then he saw her walking down the center of the ramp. You couldn't miss her.

She *was* beautiful. Jet black hair, of course. And a lithe figure. She had to be—what? Late twenties? Early thirties?

Jesse held up the FBI sign. Masumi's eyes quickly darted toward it. A big smile blossomed on her face as she headed for Jesse.

"You must be…?"

"Jesse. Jesse Striker," he said as he held out his hand.

"The author?"

Maybe she is a beauty who loves authors?

"Guilty as charged."

"I've read all your books."

"Really?"

"Yes. I love suspense and thriller novels. But, can I be honest?"

"Sure."

"I could do without the Christianity."

Not sure how best to respond, Jesse said, "Well, just glad you're reading them." Following a moment of awkward silence, Jesse said, "Luggage?"

"Yes."

"Follow me."

Twenty minutes later, Jesse and Masumi stepped through the front doors and onto the sidewalk. Before them were at least ten cabs.

"I'm parked over...there," he said, pointing in the direction of parking lot A.

Just then, a tall, heavily tattooed guy in biker rags bumped into Jesse. "Watch where you're goin'," he said, a scowl etched on his craggy face.

"Watch where...*I'm* going. I Think you've got that backwards, bud," Jesse said, looking up at the tall biker. He had to be, what—six-four? Or more?

"You some kind of smart a__? I oughta punch you out, man!"

"You ought to punch *me* out?" Jesse said. "Maybe... you ought to try."

The biker immediately threw a punch in Jesse's direction. In a blur of a second, Jesse blocked it, spun around and did a spinning side kick into the biker's mid-section.

36

The blow lifted him off the ground. He doubled over and crumbled to the pavement.

As Jesse stood over him, he was struck with the obvious. This wasn't an accident. Someone sent him. And that someone had to be Ironman. That meant that he must still be running the ex-cons from inside the Georgia State Prison.

As a small crowd began to gather, Masumi pulled a billfold from her purse and flipped it open, revealing her FBI badge.

Soon, the crowd dispersed. "I'm impressed," Masumi said. "Tae-Kwon-Do?"

Jesse nodded.

Masumi flashed Jesse a warm smile, allowing her eyes to linger a little longer than a casual, uninterested person might.

"Lead on," she said, as she grasped his arm.

*   *   *

A week later.

Friday evening

6:15 p.m.

Standing in front of the backyard grill, spatula in hand, Larry Harrelson turned to his newest recruit, Masumi Takara. "So, tell me something about yourself? I know you're from California. Berkeley. Right?"

As his newest FBI recruit, Masumi was the guest of honor. Also present at the Harrelson home were the two other agents assigned to the Knoxville Office, Bob Peterson and Randy McGill. Harrelson had also invited Billy and Jesse. Billy, because he was his best friend, and because, as a private investigator, he occasionally assisted the FBI. And Jesse, at least in part, because of a skill he had honed in writing crime and suspense fiction. Profiling. On more than one occasion, Agent Harrelson had unofficially sought his help.

"Well, you already know about all there is to know," Masumi said in answer to Agent Harrelson's question. "I'm single. Thirty-five. After a brief career as a psychologist, I got an opportunity to join the FBI. I don't want to brag, but I graduated with honors at Quantico. But, you know that. And I hate crime and I love to catch bad guys."

As Masumi's eyes panned the gathering, she squinted in Jesse's direction. "Is that Jesse Striker?"

"One and the same."

"Masumi smiled at Agent Harrelson and said, "Excuse me." She then rose, walked over and sat on the bench next to Jesse.

"We meet again," she said. She cast Jesse a flirtatious smile, and added, "If we keep meeting like this, people are going to talk." She then cocked her head coquettishly and said, "Would that be okay with you?"

Not knowing what to say, Jesse opted to say nothing. He just smiled. Masumi filled the brief void. "Why are you here? I mean, I'm glad you are. Do you have some connection with the FBI?"

"Yes…and no. I write crime suspense novels, as you know. And, believe it or not, Agent Harrelson occasionally asks for my opinion on some cases."

"You're an…amateur crime profiler?"

"That might be stretching it a bit. Probably the greater reason I'm here is Anna, Agent Harrelson's wife. She's the head librarian of the Knoxville Public Library. On several occasions, she has invited me to speak."

"Where do you write?"

"Where? Usually in my home office. But sometimes, I go to the Library."

Before Musumi could ask another question, Agent Peterson walked over to where Jesse and Masumi were seated. "Don't mean to interrupt, but, I'm Agent Peterson. Bob Peterson," he said as he held out his hand to Musumi.

Bob was five-seven, had a medium build, and wore John Lennon glasses. He was the FBI's IT man, aka— geek. But lest anyone be fooled, he was their best shooter. He was what one might call, a "double" threat.

As Bob and Musumi continued getting acquainted, Jesse glanced at Billy. He was in his default mode. Quiet. Only when he got to know someone well did he open up. Not that he was ever loquacious, but he definitely became more engaged. At such times, one would be surprised to discover his subtle humor.

Cutting off her conversation with Bob, Masumi turned to Jesse. She rose, touched him on the shoulder, and said, "See ya." She then threw him another warm, lingering smile and added, "I hope."

Masumi then walked over to Billy and sat on the picnic bench beside him. "Agent Harrelson tells me you're Cherokee, right?"

Billy nodded.

"Me too. Well...not Cherokee. Navaho. My great, great grandmother lived in northeastern Arizona. I'm 1/16th Navaho. Can't you tell?"

Billy smiled. "Now that I look more closely, yeah... it shows."

This time, Masumi smiled.

"Welcome to Tennessee!" Billy reached out his hand and Masumi buried hers in his. "I think you'll love it here."

Agent McGill who had been listening to Masumi and Billy's conversation joined them. "Ditto," he said. "I look forward to working with you."

McGill was African American. He was born and raised in Chattanooga. More times than not, his bald pate gave rise to a "You-look- just-like-Michael-Jordan" comment. Which he did. Somewhat. However, at five-ten, he was a good eight inches shorter than America's number one, six-foot-six basketball star.

An hour later, after they had consumed the last hamburger and hot dog, and had eaten the last s'more, the conversation turned to Ironman and his gang's recent attempts to intimidate Billy and Jesse's families. Jesse shared the incident at the airport.

"Here's the sad part," Harrelson said. "I'm afraid there's more to come." He looked first at Billy, then Jesse, and said, "I'll be praying."

Both Billy and Jesse were surprised to hear those words coming from Knoxville's FBI bureau chief. In the time they had known him, they had never seen anything to suggest he was a man of prayer. Or even a Christian, for that matter.

They knew he went to church. At least when the Easter lilies or poinsettias were out. And the church he and Anna attended was one of those, 'believe-whatever-you-want' types. *The Bible **is** the Word of God. The Bible **isn't** the Word of God. Jesus **is** the only way to heaven. Jesus **isn't** the only way to heaven.*

Billy personally knew their head Elder. He didn't even believe there *was* a heaven.

Even so, Billy said "Thanks Larry. We appreciate that."

"You'll let us know if anything else happens?"

"Count on it."

CHAPTER 10

Saturday.

8:00 p.m.

The Whiteclouds and Strikers worshiped at Fellowship Church in Knoxville. One of their many ministries was a once-a-month, mothers-night-out. Woya and Melissa were spending theirs at Allan's Steak House in Old Town Knoxville. Located at the northeast corner of the city's downtown area, it was originally a tough, crime-ridden section of town called "The Bowery." Revitalized in the 1980's and the 1990's, it now featured distinctive restaurants, bars, and shops. Though much smaller, it bore a striking resemblance to Bourbon Street in the New Orleans French Quarter.

Following Allen's famous steak, twice baked potato, and salad, Woya and Melissa savored their time away from home with a glass of Chardonnay. It was 10:30 when finally and reluctantly, they rose to leave. As they stepped through the golden-framed front doors and into the warm glow of one of the street's antique Victorian lamp posts, they looked in both directions. And—for good reason.

Some of the rougher sections of Knoxville bordered Old Town. A woman alone, or even two women, had reason for concern. Seeing few people on the streets, Woya and Melissa cautiously made their way to Allen's adjacent parking lot.

As they stood before it, they noticed maybe twenty-five or thirty cars that basked in the soft glow of a sodium vapor light. As far as they could tell, no one else was in the parking lot. Even so, as they cautiously made their way to Melissa's Jeep Wrangler, neither Woya nor Melissa spoke. With Melissa now at the driver's side door and Woya at the passenger side door, both made a final scan of the lot.

Seeing no one, Melissa put her hand on the door latch and began to open it. She stopped, took one final look at her surroundings, and then—froze when she saw a man step out from behind a car. She fired a quick glance a Woya, and then back at the man. He was about forty feet away, and—he was staring at them. He was dressed in a black, flowing robe and wore a hoodie. Buried within it was a mask. It was a distorted caricature of Edvard Munch's famous painting, "The Scream."

Both Woya and Melissa unconsciously held their breath as they quickly slipped into Melissa's jeep and locked the doors. Not wanting to waste a second fiddling with her seatbelt, Melissa fired the engine and tromped on the accelerator. The wheels spun, squealed, and then the Jeep lunged forward. It slid within ten feet of the man in black, with his skull-shaped head, wide eyes, and flaring nostrils. He was pointing an elongated finger at them as they sped off the parking lot.

Melissa's Jeep bounced off the edge of the curb. Her fingers blanched as she jerked the steering wheel to her right, causing the Jeep to skid sideways. The engine whined as Melissa put as much distance as she could between them and the man in black.

*   *   *

A week later.
Saturday.
9:30 a.m.
After an unfruitful all-night stakeout with agent McGill, Masumi said good-bye and slid into her black Mazda Miata convertible. Exhausted, she sat for a moment, closed her eyes, and drew in a deep breath. She then turned the ignition and began to back out. She headed for her apartment. *A nice warm shower and a nap. That's what she needed.* But then she had another thought. *I wonder...? Maybe Jesse would be at the library. He said he often wrote there.*

There was something about Jesse. She really liked him. A lot.

Motivated by that thought, she turned the car around and headed for the Knoxville Public library. She arrived ten minutes later, parked, and entered through the thick, double oak doors. She stood and let her eyes scan the surroundings. She then began walking through the library until she spotted Jesse. He was seated in a cubicle, typing away on his laptop.

"Hey," she said as she stood before him.

Surprised to see Masumi, he stopped typing, leaned back in the chair, and looked up at her. "Hey yourself. What are you doing here? Looking for a book?"

"No. Looking for you." Masumi pulled up a nearby chair and sat across from Jesse. "What are you working on?"

Suspicious of Masumi's intentions, he said, "Just…a new novel. I'm on a tight deadline and…no offense…but I don't have time to visit. You mind?"

"No…not at all," she lied. "Well, I just wanted to see you again."

Masumi rose. "Maybe we can get together when we both have more time."

Jesse didn't respond. He just looked at Masumi as she leaned forward and kissed him on the cheek. "See ya," she said, and then turned to leave.

Jesse's eyes followed her as she walked away. He didn't like what he was feeling. Obviously, Masumi was coming on to him. It was flattering, and he admitted, tempting, but—

*   *   *

Early Monday morning.

It was piercing and persistent. Just what it was, she couldn't tell. She was still lost in that subconscious state we call sleep, where the mind defrags itself to prepare for another day. But its persistence reached inside her mind

45

and dragged her from the subconscious to the conscious. Woya's eyes popped open.

It was—the phone. It rang once—twice—a third time.

Woya rolled her head toward Billy. She nudged him. When he didn't respond, she whispered, "Billy. Wake up."

He sat up on his elbows and cocking his head toward Woya, he said, "What is it?"

"The phone."

Billy quickly shifted his gaze from Woya to the alarm clock on the night stand nearest him. It was 3:00 a.m. "Who could be calling at this hour?"

Not expecting an answer, Billy threw off the covers and stood. He padded to the living room phone, lifted the receiver, and said, "Who is it?"

But—there was no response. Just silence. Dead air. And the faint sound of breathing. And then, whoever it was, clicked off.

Billy did his best to dismiss it as a mistaken or maybe a crank call. Being a PI, he had made his share of enemies. Stepping on toes was one of the downsides of his profession. That, and having them respond with a dirty look, a few choice words, and sometimes, even a crank call in the night.

Now awake, Billy stepped down the hall to the kitchen. He opened the refrigerator and took out a bottle of water. He stepped up to the sink, glanced out the window, and was about to take a swig when—

What the...?

Billy set the bottle down, and with both hands on the counter top, he leaned forward and peered out the window. There, at the far end of his lot stood a man in black. He had a hoodie pulled over his head and—*what was it...?*

Something—white. A mask? Like, a distorted carica-ture of— "The Scream!"

And he was holding something to his ear. And then—once again, the Whitecloud's phone rang.

CHAPTER 11

Tuesday.

4:30 a.m.

Moonlight passed through Abigail's bedroom window, causing squares of light to filter through the muntins. They rested on her bed and face. They jiggled and danced as a light breeze gently shook the curtains.

Being fast asleep, Abigail wasn't even aware. But then, she heard something. What was it? It sounded like, like—tapping. Her subconscious mind suggested it was a woodpecker. But as the tapping continued, it gradually tugged her awake.

Whatever it was, it wasn't a woodpecker.

And it was tapping on her window.

Abigail slipped out of the covers. She cautiously stepped on the hardwood floor and slowly tiptoed toward the window. And then—

SHE SCREAMED!

Someone was staring at her through the window. He was dressed in black. A hoodie covered a twisted, wide-eyed, image of a man screaming!

Abigail backed toward the bed. She fell on it and scrambled to the headboard. She yanked the covers up around her neck and let out another scream.

Seconds later, Jesse and Melissa raced into Abigail's bedroom. "WHAT IS IT?" Jesse asked.

Abigail said nothing. She just pointed to the window.

Jesse ran up to it and looked out, just in time to see a man in black running down his front yard toward the road, a black flowing robe silently flapping behind him.

*   *   *

Wednesday morning.

7:00 a.m.

Jesse pressed Billy's speed dial number. He answered on the second ring.

"Are you up?" Jesse asked.

"What do you think?"

"Up."

Before Billy could respond, Jesse asked, "Did Woya tell you about what happened at Allen's?"

"Yeah."

Jesse then told Billy about the man in black who tapped on Abigail's window. "It's got to be the same guy, don't you think?"

"I'm sure."

Billy then shared the phone call he and Woya received in the middle of the night and the man in black who appeared in his back yard.

"I think we both know who's behind this." Jesse said.

"Ironman. No doubt about it."

"So…what do you want to do?" Jesse asked.

49

"I think we ought to pay a visit to Warden Cartwright. Tell him what's going on. I'm sure he has ways of making Ironman back off."

"Sounds good. When?"

"I'll give him a call and see when he's free. I'll call you back."

After discovering that the warden could meet with them on Saturday, Billy called Jesse. "We're on for Saturday. Can you make it?"

"Billy, I write every day. Monday through Saturday. But…I'm my own boss. I'll just…give myself the day off."

* * *

Saturday.

9:00 a.m.

Billy was up at 8:00. Following breakfast with Woya and the kids, he went to his office, got out a map and checked the distance to Georgia State Prison. From the Wears Valley / Gatlinburg area, where he and Jesse lived, it was 367 miles. It would take over five hours to get there. Had he realized that when he was talking to the warden, he would have chosen to just call him. Fortunately, it wasn't too late. Confident Jesse would agree, Billy picked up his cell phone and punched in his number.

"Are you up?"

"I am."

"You know, if we drive to the prison, it's going to be a ten hour day. Five hours there and five hours back, not counting what time we spend with the warden. I'm guessing that would be…five or ten minutes at the most. I was thinking that maybe, I should just give him a call. What do you think?"

"Well, as much as I would like to spend ten hours in a car, bonding with you, I opt for you making a call."

"Okay, I'll do it. As soon as I know something, I'll get back to you."

Billy said goodbye and immediately placed a call to Georgia State Prison and the warden. Cartwright answered on the first ring.

"This is Warden Cartwright, how can I help you?"

"Warden, this is Billy Whitecloud…"

"Before Billy could state the reason for his call, the warden said, "Billy, great to hear from you. I'm looking forward to meeting with you and Jesse. It's been a long time. About…ten years?"

"Twelve, actually, but if you don't mind, I think we can accomplish the same thing on the phone."

"That's fine with me. What do you need?"

"Well, it's about Ironman."

Billy shared what was going on. "We wondered if you could apply a little pressure to get him to back off. You know, restrict his visits, phone calls… whatever."

"I can do better than that. It's been a while since he's been in the hole."

The hole was another name for solitary confinement.

"Ironman's got a bad case of claustrophobia. I could give him a couple days to think about what he's doing. And…if that doesn't work, I can promise him a month. I think that would do the trick."

"Warden, we'd really appreciate that. That would give us and our families a little peace of mind."

"Consider it done," the warden said, "Is that all you need?"

"Yes, sir. That should do it. Thanks!"

Billy said goodbye and called Jesse. "Mission accomplished," he said. "The warden's going to put Ironman in the hole and let him think about what he's doing.

"Well, here's hoping it works. If not, it just might be like poking a pit bull with a stick."

*　*　*

Early Monday morning.

Ironman lasted one day in solitary. "GET ME OUT OF HERE!" he yelled at the guard, kicking and banging on the solid metal door. The guard opened the ten-by-ten inch thick panel. "What do you want?"

"OUT! CALL THE WARDEN!"

Aware that Ironman's stay was to be intentionally short, the guard pressed his lapel mike and spoke to Warden Cartwright. Less than twenty minutes later, Ironman was back in his cell, fuming. More than ever, once and for all—he was determined to get even with Whitecloud and Striker.

CHAPTER 12

Monday evening.

It was 8:00 p.m. when the Striker's phone rang. Melissa answered, "Hello."

"Is this Ms. Striker? Melissa Striker?"

"It is."

"Ms. Striker, my name is Clarice. Clarice Paine. I'm a Social Worker at Erlanger Hospital. In Chattanooga."

Melissa sucked in a quick breath. Her father lived in Chattanooga. He was eighty-five and had suffered two heart attacks.

"Is this about my dad? Edward Grafton?"

"It is. I'm afraid he's had another attack. He's in ICU. Is it possible for you to come."

"Absolutely!"

Melissa hung up and yelled for Jesse. He was in his study. From the sound of her voice, there was a problem of some kind. He quickly saved what he had been working on, and hurried to the living room. "What is it?"

"It's dad. He's had another heart attack. He's in intensive care at Erlanger. I need to go there. Now."

"I agree. You want me to come?"

"No…no…you need to deal with this Ironman thing. If I need you, I'll call."

"What about Abby?"

"I'm going to take her. It could be the last time she would see her grandpa. I pray not, but...you never know."

An hour later, at 9:00 p.m., Melissa and Abigail stood by the front door, ready to leave.

"Let's pray," Jesse said. Melissa and Abigail set down their suitcases and the three joined hands. *"Father God, please look over dad. I know he's had a good, long life. Forgive us for being selfish, but please, grant him several more years. And Lord, guide Melissa and Abby safely to Chattanooga, and use them to comfort dad. We ask it all in Jesus blessed name, amen."*

Jesse kissed Melissa and gave Abigail a hug. He picked up their luggage and carried it to Melissa's Jeep. "Be careful," he said as they entered the car. Jesse was standing by the driver's side door. He touched his lips with two fingers and pressed them on the window. Melissa did the same from inside the car, then started the engine. Seconds later, she and Abigail were on their way.

Jesse stood, staring at the taillights until he could no longer see them. He then walked back inside, and for a second time, said a prayer. He returned to his study. He had barely sat down when the phone rang.

"Hello."

"This is Masumi. I...I need to talk to you."

"What about?"

"I...can't say on the phone."

"Where are you?"

"Pete's."

"At Pete's? The bar?"

"Yeah," she slurred.

"You've been drinking?"

"Only a little. But I do need to talk to you. Will you come?"

Jesse knew better. If someone's in trouble, you need to help, right? But there are times when saying "no" is the wiser response.

Jesse had once received a call from a transient. He said he needed a few dollars for a meal. Jesse met him at a motel. He knocked on the door and entered. A heavy, wide-shouldered man stepped within inches of his face, and said, "How much money you got?"

Jesse shook his head and turned to leave when the man put a hand on his shoulder. Instinctively, Jesse spun around and sent a fist crashing into the man's nose. From that day forward, Jesse wasn't quick to say, "yes" when someone asked for help. At the same time, his faith didn't allow him to totally ignore someone who might need it.

There was silence on the line, then Masumi said, "Will you? Will you come talk to me?"

Jesse reluctantly agreed. Thirty minutes later, he entered Pete's. It was an upscale bar. There were, he guessed, maybe forty there, some sitting on stools facing the bartender, others in booths. He stood and scanned the place looking for Masumi. She was in a booth in the far corner. She stood, wobbled a little, and waved at him.

As he began walking toward the booth, Jesse whispered a short prayer—*"God help me."*

Masumi was still standing when Jesse stepped up to the booth. She threw her arms around him. Jesse immediately pushed her away and gently ushered her into the seat.

"What's this about, Masumi?"

"You," she slurred, "and me."

"What?"

"I…I like you, Jesse."

"Masumi, I'm married. Happily married."

"So…"

"So, I don't fool around."

"Why?"

"Are you kidding?"

"No, lot's of married men fool around."

"Yeah…that's probably true. But, I'm not one of them."

Again, the same question, "Why?"

"You want to know the real reason?"

"Yeah."

"I'm a Christian."

Masumi said nothing at first. She just cocked her head to one side, squinted, and said, "You're kidding, right? I mean, I know you put some Christianity in your novels, but I thought that was just your shtick. I didn't think anyone believed that anymore."

"Believe it." Thirty seconds of awkward silence followed. Jesse filled it saying, "Do you even know what a Christian is, Masumi?"

"Apparently not. Tell me."

Being inebriated, Jesse didn't know if Masumi could even comprehend what he was about to say. But, she had said, 'tell me,' so—he did. He shared the truth that we all are flawed sinners, separated from God and heaven, but that God loves us nonetheless. He shared that God sent his son Jesus to earth to earn for us a place in heaven by His perfect life and by his death on a cross—and that He promised forgiveness and eternal life to all who believed that and trusted in His Son.

When he had finished, Masumi was still staring at him. She shook her head, then said, "You really believe that nonsense?"

"Yes, Masumi. I do."

"Well, I don't. I guess I made a mistake about you."

"I guess you did," Jesse said as Masumi rose on unsteady feet.

Jesse was immediately conflicted. Masumi shouldn't drive. Should he give her a ride home? That, he considered, might give Masumi the wrong idea.

"Masumi, sit back down. You're in no condition to drive. I'll call a cab."

Masumi sat and glared glassy-eyed at Jesse. She waited a few minutes, finished her drink in silence, then rising, staggered toward the front door.

As soon as she left, Jesse bowed his head and prayed that God would get her safely home.

CHAPTER 13

Masumi stepped out the front door of Pete's as the cab pulled up. She ignored it. Instead, she looked to her left, then her right, trying to remember where she had parked her car. Gradually, a few synapses of her mind, not yet dulled by alcohol, came to her rescue. Her Miata was in the parking lot beside Pete's.

Were she sober, she would have been embarrassed. Since she wasn't, she simply wobbled her way onto the dim parking lot. She stopped beside her Miata, reached in her purse, and fumbled for her keys. It took longer than usual to find them. When she did, Masumi pulled them out only to drop them on the blacktop. Feeling dizzy, like maybe she was about to faint, Masumi nonetheless bent over, picked up her keys, and attempted to insert her car key in the door lock.

She succeeded on the third try, opened the door, and slipped behind the steering wheel. With her eyes intently locked on the ignition, to her amazement, she was able to insert the key on the first try. She started her Miata.

Had she been able to see the unseeable, she would have known that someone was in the car with her. Someone big. Someone with long flowing hair and light blue eyes. He was sitting in the passenger seat, staring at her. It was Adryel.

Masumi backed up her Miata, only to hear the sound of crunching metal. She had struck the front of a nearby Lexis. In her present state, she was neither fully aware of what she had done, nor did she care. She just shook her head in a vain attempt to regain her shifting focus. Though unsuccessful, she nonetheless put the car in drive. It lurched forward and bounded on the street. Fortunately, given the hour, Hamilton Avenue was empty.

The white center line shifted from her left to her right and then totally disappeared as Masumi's hands slipped off the steering wheel. She slumped to her right, unconscious. To anyone glancing at the passing Miata, it would appear driverless.

Adryel immediately took over. He quickly plucked her comatose body from the driver's seat. He set her where he had been, moved behind the wheel and took control of her Miata.

At the corner of Anderson and Holt, Masumi's seemingly driverless car passed a parked police car, causing the officer to do a double take and nearly drop his Starbucks in his lap.

He squinted out the driver's side window, staring at the diminishing taillights of the black Miata as it accurately maneuvered itself down the road and around a corner.

He would have given chase, but—how would he explain that he had stopped a driverless car. What would he say in his report? *This evening at 10:40, I approached a black Miata driving down the road with no one behind the wheel.*

Adryel drove Masumi's car to her duplex and pulled up the drive. He stopped the car, got out, and walked to the passenger side door. He opened it, lifted Masumi's limp body from the Miata, and carried her to her front door.

Masumi's neighbor, eighty-five-year-old George Henderson, lived with his wife Ruth in an adjacent Victorian home. He had just finished his fourth bottle of five percent Redds Ale, and was about to get his sixth when he heard Masumi's car pull onto her drive.

He stumbled up to his side window and squinting, peered out. His eyebrows rose as he watched Masumi's body floating up to and through her front door that had seemingly opened all by itself. "Ruth," he slurred, "You're not going to believe this."

Once inside, Adryel gently set Masumi's body on her bed. He laid a blanket over her, and left. George, who was still standing by the window, looked on wide-eyed as, once again, Masumi's front door opened, then closed—all by itself.

* * *

Tuesday.

8:30 p.m.

His phone privileges restored, Ironman placed a call to Sanchez.

"What do you want?" Sanchez said.

"I want you here tomorrow. And I want you to bring Snake."

"What time?"

"Visiting hours are 10 to Noon and 1:00 to 4:00. Be here by 2:00."

"Okay. We'll be there."

"You d___ well better be."

* * *

Wednesday.

2:00 p.m.

As Ironman, Sanchez and Snake sat at a table for four in the visitors' room, Sanchez shared their intimidations of Billy, Jesse and their families.

Ironman smiled and nodded to show his approval.

"What do you want us to do next?" Sanchez asked.

"Something bigger. Much bigger."

"Like…what?"

"I want you to get me out of here."

Both Sanchez and Snake leaned back. Then Sanchez said, "How in the h__ are we supposed to do that?"

"I've been thinking," Ironman said. "I've got a fool proof plan."

Sanchez and Snake looked at each other in disbelief. Then looking back at Ironman, Snake skeptically said, "Really?"

"Really." Ironman glanced around the room, stared momentarily at the two guards, then whispered, "This is what you're going to do."

After hearing Ironman's plan, Sanchez and Snake once again looked at each other, then back at Ironman. "You know," Snake said, "that just might work."

"Okay," Sanchez said to Ironman. "Give me a little time to put it together. I'll gather the guys at the cabin, fill them in, and we'll plan the escape. I'll get word to you when we're ready to pull it off."

CHAPTER 14

Sunday evening.

6:45 p.m.

It was the Strikers' turn to host the weekly Whitecloud/Striker Sunday evening gathering. There wasn't a cloud in the sky as the sun began to slip behind the tops of the Virginia and loblolly pines that fronted Jesse and Melissa's cabin. Flowering rhododendron and a smattering of mountain laurel dominated the drop off, fifty feet beyond the back porch. And the smell of charcoal was in the air as Billy, Woya, and their children pulled up the Strikers' driveway.

By 7:00, they were all seated on one of the two picnic tables that rested on the backyard teardrop patio. The adults—Billy, Woya, Jesse and Melissa sat on one. The kids—fair skinned, blue-eyed Abigail Striker with her Scandinavian blond hair and her best friends, Chloe and Nathan Whitecloud, sat on the other. To look at, they were as different as could be. With their raven hair and dark brown eyes, Chloe and Nathan were as true a reflection of their parents as Abigail was of hers.

"How's your father?" Woya asked Melissa.

"He's fine. Thanks for asking."

Melissa shared that her father got out of ICU on Wednesday, was in a room that same day, and that she took him home on Thursday.

At 8:30, after eating their fill of hamburgers and hot-dogs, they all gathered around the fire and toasted marsh-mallows. Twenty minutes later, Abigail said, "Can we play a game, Uncle Billy?"

Technically speaking, Billy was not Abigail's uncle, but to her, Jesse and Melissa, he was that and more. Besides rooming together in college, both Billy and Jesse had excelled in sports—Billy as a tight end for the Vols, and Jesse as the UTK's top gymnast. They quickly became best friends.

Their friendship grew even more when Jesse married Billy's sister, Jenny. Her tragic death had drawn them even closer. And to Jesse, there was no one quite like Billy. As the cliché goes, he was "a force to be reckoned with."

At one of the Whitecloud/Striker gatherings at Billy and Woya's Gatlinburg home, they were all confronted by a black bear that had wandered into their backyard. It had been drawn by the scent of steak Billy was cooking on the grill.

Everyone jumped off the picnic bench and backed toward the cabin. Everyone except Billy. He calmly rose, started yelling at the bear, and chased him away. From that day forward, to Abigail, Billy was her "Samson."

That he was Cherokee and wore his hair long in the manner of his ancestors only added to his mystique in Abigail's eyes.

"What do you want to play?" Billy asked.

"The same game we played last week," Abigail said.

"Yeah," echoed Nathan. Chloe nodded in agreement.

The game they were referring to was one that Cherokee kids and adults had played for centuries. They would form two teams. A player from one team, then the other, would take turns palming an object, moving it quickly from one hand to the other to a drumbeat. When the drum stopped, members of the other team would guess what hand the object was in.

In decades past, Cherokee adults who guessed correctly would win a piece of land, a horse or, in some cases, female companionship.

Billy had altered the game for present company. While everyone pounded a drumbeat on the table, one team would guess which hand held the hidden object. If they were correct, they received a point. At the end, the team with the most points would ask the losing team to do something silly. It could be walking around and clucking like chickens or anything else that came to mind.

For the next thirty minutes, the adult table challenged the kids. As it turns out, the kids won. In the time that followed, the adults continued to visit. Bored, Nathan turned to Abigail and Chloe and said, "Hey, you want to play hide- and-seek?"

Abigail, who would never go to bed unless a light was on, quickly said, "It's too dark." At 9:30, it was dark. And the sliver of moon did nothing to negate that, since its minimal light could not filter through the thick woods that surrounded the Strikers' cabin. So, for Abigail, hiding in the woods was a non-starter.

But the darkness wasn't her greatest concern. Abigail had a severe case of asthma. Any kind of stress, especially physical, like running—as she certainly would have to do were they to play hide-and-seek—could trigger an episode. She had on too many occasions experienced gasping for air like a fish out of water to want to chance it.

"I don't want to," she said.

Chloe played the arbiter. "We could do it for maybe just a half hour," she said. "After that, maybe we could play your new video game, *Michael*. Would that be okay?"

Michael was a Christian video game where the archangel Michael warred against demons.

That Chloe would make that suggestion would have been a surprise for anyone who didn't know her well. Though taller than Abigail and Nathan, she was by nature, shy. In the classroom, she would speak only when called on. On the playground, she would sit on the sidelines while others played. There was one exception. When she knew someone well, and trusted them, she was surprisingly talkative. And persuasive. And she knew Nathan and Abigail well.

"Come on, Abby. Let's do it for a half hour. Okay? Then we can go inside and play your video game."

Abigail reluctantly agreed.

Melissa, who had overheard the children's conversation, fired a glance at her daughter. "Don't run, Abby," she warned.

"I won't," Abigail said, knowing all along that wouldn't be possible.

For the next twenty minutes, everything seemed fine. Billy, Woya, Jesse and Melissa could hear the occasional "Here I come, ready or not," and the laughter when someone was found.

And then…it happened.

CHAPTER 15

Nathan and Chloe were searching for Abigail. "Leotie, is that you?" Nathan asked as he saw his sister about fifteen feet away.

Billy and Woya had given Chloe and Nathan Cherokee middle names. Nathan's was "Waya." It means "wolf." Chloe's was Leotie, which is Cherokee for "Flower of the Prairie."

"I can't fine her anywhere," Nathan said.

"Me neither."

"Listen," Nathan said. You hear that?"

"Hear what?"

"Breathing. I hear someone breathing."

Those were the last words Nathan spoke. With Chloe close behind, he cautiously walked in the direction of the sound and soon—he found Abigail. She was lying on the ground, gasping for breath.

Nathan screamed, "MOM…DAD!" Nathan spun around and began racing for the cabin. Chloe was right behind him.

Seconds later, Nathan was at the cabin. "IT'S… ABIGAIL!" he yelled.

Billy, Woya, Jesse, and Melissa jumped out of their seats."

"WHAT IS IT? WHAT'S WRONG?" Jesse asked.

"She…she…she can't breathe!"

"WHERE IS SHE?" Jesse asked. Without answering, Nathan turned and raced back into the woods. Jesse and Melissa followed him. Billy and Woya were close behind.

*　*　*

As Abigail lay struggling for each breath, she felt a presence. Someone had knelt beside her. He was big. Real big. He had long, black hair and was wearing a shining white robe. One big hand gently opened her mouth and then, from a foot away, he blew into it.

She could see it. It was like—like glowing blue air, but it glittered, like maybe it had silver sparkles in it. Once the air entered her mouth, she could breathe. She gulped in several big breaths and then slowly sat up. Her voice quivered as she stared wide eyed at the person who was now towering over her. "Who are you?"

The big man looked down on Abigail. He smiled, said, "I am Adryel," and then—disappeared.

*　*　*

When Jesse and Melissa reached Abigail, she was standing. "Are you okay?" Jesse asked.

"I'm…I'm fine, but…"

Abigail didn't finish the sentence. Stunned by what had happened, she just stood there, trembling.

"Let me carry you back to the cabin," Jesse said.

"I'm okay, Dad. I can walk."

When they arrived at the cabin, they sat on the picnic tables. Abigail relayed what had happened. She described the man who had helped her breathe.

Jesse and Melissa, Billy and Woya exchanged glances, then Jesse recited a passage from Scripture. It was from the first chapter of the book of Hebrews, *"Are not all angels ministering spirits sent to serve those who will inherit salvation?"*

Billy smiled and said, "Praise God!" At Jesse's lead, they all held hands, and one after another, each of them thanked God for sending an angel to heal Abigail. They all closed with an "amen," and hugged one another.

CHAPTER 16

Tuesday afternoon.

3:00 p.m.

Masumi sat in her Miata outside the Knoxville Public Library. When she first arrived and parked, she had no way of knowing whether Jesse would be there. She breathed a sigh of relief when she saw his Cobalt. She desperately wanted to set things straight. Apologize. She would have prayed for the right words but, when you don't believe, that's obviously not an option.

Ten minutes passed.

Fifteen.

Then she saw him coming out of the library. She stepped out of her Miata, walked beside his Cobalt, and waited for him. Surprised to see her, Jesse's brows furrowed as he stopped three feet from Masumi.

"Can we talk?" Masumi said.

Jesse hesitated briefly, then said, "Sure."

"I…I want to apologize. The last time I saw you, I was, you know, a little inebriated. Correction. A lot inebriated. Anyway, I'm sorry I came on to you like I did. It was stupid. I also apologize for what I said about your faith. I just don't believe any of it, but there was no excuse for saying what I did."

Masumi and Jesse's eyes locked. A few seconds later, seeming much longer, slipped by. "Do you forgive me?"

Before Jesse could respond, she added, "That's pretty big with Christians, right?"

Jesse gave Masumi a warm smile. "Right. Of course I forgive you," he said, reaching out his hand. She took it, but lest he think she had any ulterior motives, she quickly let go.

"Masumi," Jesse said, "I know you don't believe. There was a time when I didn't either. Like you, I had a lot of misconceptions about Christians." Jesse paused, then said, "Will you do me a favor...?"

"Anything," she said, quickly adding, "Almost."

"Would you consider coming to church with Melissa and me? Just once?"

"Once?

"Once."

"Okay. Thanks, Jesse," Masumi said as she spun around and took a couple steps toward her car. She stopped, turned back and said, "You know, Jesse, I really would like to believe."

Masumi then shrugged her shoulders, slipped into her Miata, and backed out of her parking spot. Without looking at Jesse, she reached her hand out the driver's side window and waved as she sped away.

* * *

Wednesday evening.

8:00 p.m.

"Listen up," Sanchez said to the eleven members of the Georgia Ex-Cons. They had all gathered at Ironman's secluded cabin, nestled deep in the woods of north Georgia. It was located forty miles from Macon.

In the early twentieth century, it had been a popular vacation spot. At that time, four cabins, each capable of housing twenty guests, were fronted by a spring-fed pond. Only one cabin remained—the other three had succumbed to decades of neglect and vegetation.

Even the road to Ironman's cabin had, for the most part, been taken over by undergrowth. The only way in was a narrow, winding logging road. It ended in a turn-around about a mile from the cabin. From there, one had to either walk or ride a four-wheeler or motorcycle down a narrow, rutted path.

The cabin was once owned by the former senator of Vermont and Ironman's discredited father, the Honorable (make that 'less-than-honorable') J. Robert Purdue. He had bequeathed the cabin to his illegitimate son, Beau Haggart.

"Me and Snake just got back from visiting the boss."

"How's he doing?" Bear asked.

"Better than expected. And…he's going to be feeling even better before too long."

"Because..?" Bear asked.

"Because…we're going to spring him."

The ex-cons looked at one another, some with eyes raised in doubt. Tall Man, who was leaning against the counter, said, "Yeah…piece of cake."

"Yeah, it is. Matter of fact. And I'll tell you why. Listen up. This is what we're going to do. We're going to kidnap the warden, his wife, and his seventeen year-old-daughter…"

"Well…that sounds easy," Tall Man interrupted.

Sanchez glared at him and said, "Shut your d___ mouth and hear me out. Like I said, we're going to kidnap the warden and his family, and…we're also going to kidnap his younger brother and his family. His brother is about the same age and size as Ironman, and get this—he's a dead ringer for him. They could be twins."

There was a pause as Sanchez let that soak in.

"I don't get it," Slow Beef said.

Sanchez slowly shook his head. "You don't get much of anything."

That was true. Slow Beef was obviously his biker name. It was given him because he was beefy, and—because he was slow. Real slow.

"Here's what we're going to do. This Friday evening, we'll kidnap both families and bring them here. Then, Saturday morning, we'll have the warden and his Ironman 'look-a-like' brother go to the prison. He'll have a ball cap on, pulled down to hide his face.

"The warden will then tell the guards that he and his brother are just dropping by his office to pick up some documents for a court appearance. Once inside, the warden will ask a guard to bring Ironman to his office. Ironman and the warden's brother will then exchange clothes—the warden's brother will put on Ironman's orange jumpsuit and Ironman will put on whatever his brother is wearing.

"Ironman will duct tape and gag the warden's brother and lock him in the office bathroom. Then, the warden and Ironman will leave the prison. As far as the guards are concerned, it's just the warden and his brother leaving.

"The warden will be instructed to bring Ironman to the rest stop near the prison. We'll meet them there, hood the warden, and bring him and Ironman to the cabin."

"Well, shut my mouth," Tall Man said. "D___. I think that just might work."

CHAPTER 17

Friday.

6:45 p.m.

Twelve year old Madison was standing in the middle of the two acre front yard of her family's two-story, colonial home in Knoxville. She was playing with the family's Border Collie, Ranger.

A salmon sky was just settling over the tree tops. It would disappear in roughly a half hour. A light breeze rustled the leaves of the tulip, wild cherry and bitternut hickory trees that lined the perimeter of her home. It caused the forty-year old redbuds that stretched their limbs between them, reaching for a bit of sunshine, to gently sway in the breeze. A whiff of seventy-degree air periodically lifted her shoulder-length, brown hair, and the smell of newly mown grass lightly scented the air.

Supper was over. Her father, thirty-eight year old Seth Cartwright, was in his office surfing the internet. Her mother, Andrea was clearing the dinner table and putting dishes in the dishwasher.

Ranger, who had just returned with a stick that Madison had thrown, was eagerly wagging his tail for an encore, until—

He heard a sound that made him uneasy. He dropped the stick. His head snapped in the direction of the twisting, tree-lined, quarter-mile drive that led to the Seth Cartwright home. Seconds later, Madison froze and stared in the same direction.

She couldn't see anything.

Not yet.

But she could hear it. It was a deep, rumbling sound. The kind Harleys make. And clearly, they were headed for her home.

But why?

The secluded Cartwright home seldom had visitors. The few that dropped by usually did so by invitation. Or, at the very least, they were family or friends. But strangers? Rarely did they enter the winding, graveled road to the Seth Cartwright home. The words PRIVATE DRIVE and the ADT sign discouraged the uninvited and unknown.

Suddenly—

The rumbling became a roar as, one after another, nine Harleys appeared at the end of the drive. They were still a good distance away, but they were definitely speeding toward her home. Fast. They were led by a black GMC van with blacked out windows.

Madison spun around and raced for the porch. She bounded up the steps and yelled, "MOM! DAD!"

Andrea had already heard the sound. She stopped wiping her hands on a dish towel, leaned forward, and stared out the kitchen window. Her eyes still locked on the van and the fast approaching cycles, she yelled, "SETH!"

Secluded in his office, Seth Cartwright—CPA and younger brother of Warden, Roland Cartwright—hadn't heard the sounds. He did, however, hear his wife. From the sound of it, something bad had happened, or—was about to happen. He jumped out of his seat.

"WHAT IS IT?" he yelled as he joined Andrea and Madison at their screen door. He held his breath and stared out as, one after another, the van and the Harleys pulled up in front of their home and shut off their engines.

As the low level dust from the rock drive slowly settled, two bikers sauntered up the steps of the front porch.

Without looking at Andrea or Madison, Seth whispered, "Get in the upstairs bedroom, and…lock the door. Now!"

A few seconds later, the bikers stepped up to the front door. "Mr. Cartwright, I presume?" said one. He had an accent. Mexican, probably. Certainly Latino.

"Yes? What do you want?"

"You," he said, and he pulled open the screen door and stepped within inches of Seth's face. "And…your family."

"I don't know what you think you're doing, but I want you to get off my property. NOW!"

"Really?"

The Spanish speaking biker suddenly exploded. He shoved Seth Cartwright into the hallway wall. "GET YOUR FAMILY DOWN HERE!"

"Okay…okay…I'll get them."

Seth Cartwright turned to leave. He had taken only one step when the biker grabbed him by the collar and jerked him to a halt. "Where you think you're going man? You think I'm crazy? You think I'm going to just let you walk away and disappear to who knows where? You've probably got a gun somewhere, don't you. Hey…so do I."

The biker pulled a Glock 22 from behind his back and pointed it between Seth Cartwright's eyes. Smiling, he said, "Ask your wife and daughter to join us. Please."

Cartwright did as he was told, and a minute later, Andrea and Madison walked down the second floor steps into the hallway. Their arms were wrapped around each other."

"Well, it's good to see all of you. We've come to give you a little ride."

"Where to?" Seth asked.

"You'll find out soon enough."

CHAPTER 18

The three Cartwrights were ushered into the black van, hooded, and driven to Ironman's cabin. When they arrived, the two bikers who had stayed behind, Slow Beef and Tall Man, greeted them from the front porch.

"Well, look what the cat drug in," Tall Man said. He stepped aside as the other ex-cons ushered the Cartwrights into the living room. As Madison passed by, Tall Man cast a lecherous downward grin in her direction and gently laid a grimy palm on her head. "My, but you're a cutie."

Seth, who was directly behind his daughter said, "Get your hand off her!"

Before Tall Man could respond, the Spanish speaking man glared at him and said, "DEJARA A LA NINA SOLA!"

Seth, who spoke a little Spanish, thanked the man for telling the biker to *leave her alone*. Whoever this man was, he was obviously the leader. Had Seth any doubt, that was confirmed when the man ordered them to take a seat.

"What are you going to do with us?" Seth asked.

"I'll tell you when I'm good and ready. For now, you just do as you're told. As long as you don't try to escape, we won't tie you up. If you have to go to the bathroom, it's down the hall." The Spanish speaking man, whom they would later learn went by the name, Ricardo Sanchez, pointed in that direction.

"One of our guys will be at each door at all times, so don't even think of trying to escape." He paused, then said, "That's it. Make yourselves at home. You're gonna' be here for awhile." Then to Slow Beef, he said, "Keep an eye on 'em."

Sanchez then stepped up to Tall Man. He grabbed him by the collar, shoved him against the wall and said, "You even come close to that little girl, I swear, when I return, I'll beat the s___ out of you."

Sanchez gave Tall Man one last shove to emphasize his point, then spun around and walked toward the front door. His back to the others, he said, "Let's go get the Warden."

* * *

9:30 p.m.

Ruddy-faced and burr cut Roland Cartwright, his wife Olivia, and their seventeen-year-old daughter, Paige, lived two miles from the prison. Their forty-year old brick ranch squatted on a two acre plot in the country. Then again, given the size of Reidsville, just about every home was in the country.

There was a town. Of sorts. It consisted of a gas station, a post office, a laundromat, a local restaurant called Delilah's, and little else.

Olivia sat at the kitchen table, drinking coffee, reading *People* magazine and puffing on an e-cigarette. Warden Cartwright was in the basement putting together a four-propeller drone complete with spy camera. He bought it primarily for fun, but he had thought of periodically flying it over the prison to have a bird's eye view of the grounds.

Paige was in her bedroom, talking on her cell phone with her best friend, Kelly.

Olivia was the first to hear the Harleys. She was also the first to see them. Even from a quarter mile away, their jouncing beams sent shafts of light that dispelled the growing darkness that had enveloped the Cartwright home.

"ROLAND!"

When he didn't respond, Olivia hurried to the basement door to the left of the refrigerator, opened it, and called again. "ROLAND...YOU NEED TO COME UP HERE!"

"WHAT IS IT?" But before she could respond, he too heard the guttural growl of several Harleys. He bounded up the stairs as fast as his fifty-eight year old body would allow and passed through the kitchen and into the hallway. He had just reached the screen door when two of nine motorcycles rolled up in front of their home. Behind them was a black van.

Suspicious by nature and necessity, Roland Cartwright opened the closet door adjacent to the front door and pulled out his 20-guage shotgun.

Two bikers stepped onto the porch and up to the screen door. "Are you Roland Cartwright?"

"I am. And, who in the hell are you?"

"Let me just say," Sanchez said, "we are the ones who have kidnapped your little brother, Seth and his family."

"You WHAT?"

"I think you heard me. And...if you ever want to see them alive again, I suggest you, your wife, and your daughter come with us."

Stunned by what he had just heard, Cartwright said nothing at first. He drew a deep breath, raised his head in defiance, and said, "Come with you...where?"

"You'll find out soon enough," said Snake. He was tall, thin and had the meanest looking face Cartwright had ever seen, and he had seen a lot of mean faces.

Snake yanked open the screen door. Just as quickly, Cartwright raised his shotgun. Snake snatched the barrel and said, "I wouldn't do that if I were you. You're kind of outnumbered, if you get my drift."

Cartwright let go of the shotgun.

"Call your wife and daughter!"

CHAPTER 19

Roland Cartwright did as he was told, and soon he, Olivia, and Paige were hooded and shoved into the black van. Fifty-minutes later, the van pulled up to the narrow path off a logging road turnaround. Sanchez, who was driving the van, parked it.

At his instructions, the bikers went on ahead while he and Snake took off their captives' hoods. With Sanchez ahead and Snake behind, their jouncing flashlights leading the way, the two ex-cons and their three captives proceeded down the one mile path toward the cabin.

Given the darkness, the narrow path with its hidden roots and unseen branches, it was slow going. At best, Sanchez figured it would take them maybe thirty minutes to reach the cabin.

It was 11:30 when he, Snake, and the Roland Cartwright family finally walked up the steps of the porch. Sanchez and Snake stood by the open door as Warden Cartwright and his family entered the living room.

"Oh my God," Olivia stopped and froze as she saw Seth, Andria and Madison seated on the couch.

Before anyone could respond, Sanchez said, "SIT! ALL OF YOU!"

Roland refused. Instead, he remained standing. His chin held high, he said, "What do you think you're doing?"

Sanchez glared at him for a few seconds. He then nodded at Bear who sauntered up to the warden and shoved him into a chair beside the couch.

"What do I think I'm doing? Actually, I *know* what I'm doing."

Sanchez gave the Roland Cartwright family the same instructions he had given Seth's family. "We have no intention of hurting any of you, but don't be mistaken. If you try to escape, you'll spend the rest of your time tied to a chair. Got it?"

When none of the Cartwrights answered, he repeated himself, "GOT IT!"

They all nodded.

"Okay, here's the deal. You've asked why we kidnapped you. Here's why." To the warden and his brother Seth, he said, "You're going to help us spring Ironman."

"WHAT? You're kidding...right?" asked the warden.

"Do I look like I'm kidding? And shut your d___ mouth and listen!"

Everyone sat in stone silence as Sanchez glared at the warden. He then looked at the others and said, "Here's how it's going to work." Then to the warden he continued, "Take a good look at your brother, warden. He's a dead ringer for Ironman. They're the same size, same build... they even look alike.

"So, here's what you're going to do. Tomorrow morning, you and your brother are going to enter the prison. While your baby brother is slumping in the passenger seat, his Tennessee Titans' ball cap pulled way down, you're going to tell the guards at the gate that you and your brother are picking up some files and that you'll be back out in a half hour or so.

"Once inside your office, you're going to call for Ironman. Your brother," Sanchez said looking at Seth, then back at the warden, "...is going to put on Ironman's jumpsuit and Ironman is going to put on your brother's clothes. Ironman is then going to tie up your brother in your office bathroom, and you're going to leave with Ironman."

Sanchez paused, looked at the warden, then his brother. "Nod if you understand."

After they did, Sanchez continued, "One other thing, warden. Once you've left the prison, a couple of my guys are going to meet you at the rest stop to make sure that Ironman is with you, and that all has gone as planned."

They all sat in silence for a full ten seconds. The warden broke it when he said, "What happens then?"

"My guys will lead you and Ironman back here. Come Monday morning, we'll let you go. All of you."

Roland Cartwright looked at his brother, their families, then back at Sanchez. "Why would you do that? Why would you leave any witnesses?"

"Why? Because I don't like killing people. And because none of you will talk. Cause, you see, there are twelve of us. Thirteen counting Ironman. And if any one of us is caught, I assure you, one of us *will* kill you and your families."

The truth was, neither Sanchez nor Ironman had any intention of allowing any witnesses to live. But to insure the warden and his brother did as they were instructed, it was best they think that maybe, just maybe—they would all come out of this alive.

CHAPTER 20

Saturday morning.

9:00 a.m.

Warden Roland Cartwright squinted through the windshield to block the glare of the morning sun as he, and his Ironman "look-a-like" brother, Seth, passed through the double razor wire fence that surrounded the prison. He slowed his government issued SUV and stopped alongside the guard house.

The words on the driver's side door, GEORGIA DEPARTMENT OF CORRECTIONS and beneath it, the word WARDEN clearly identified for the guards that the boss had just arrived.

Seth was slouched in the passenger seat, his identity shielded by sunglasses and a ball cap pulled way down over his face.

"Morning," the Warden said to one of two guards who stood by the open door of the guard house, a clipboard in his hand. "How you doing, Josh?"

"Doing great, sir."

Five-foot-ten, twenty-six year old Josh McDonald was a combat veteran of the Muslim wars. He had lost a leg when attempting to defuse a land mine. Given the present economy, he felt lucky to have a job.

It wasn't his first choice. He had wanted to join the Georgia State Police. Unfortunately, his injury jinxed that. He feared he would also be rejected for the position of guard at Georgia State Prison. That he wasn't made waking up in the morning something to look forward to.

Josh limped up to the driver's window, leaned way forward, and peered at the warden, then his passenger.

"I don't think you know my brother, Josh," the warden said as he glanced at Seth, then back at the guard. "I'm afraid he's catching up on his sleep. He had a late night."

Josh squinted in Seth's direction, then stood and wrote something on his clipboard.

"We're just going to slip in," the warden said. "I need to pick up some files for court. I should be back out in about a half hour."

"Yes, sir," Josh said, and backing up a couple steps, he motioned for the warden to proceed.

Five minutes later, Warden Cartwright and Seth entered the warden's office. While Seth hid in the small office bathroom, Cartwright called the guard of C-WING to bring up Beau Haggart.

A short time later, fifty-year old Carl Willis, who had been a guard at Georgia State for going on thirty-three years, knocked on the warden's door. Beau Haggard stood beside him, shackled hand and foot.

"Carl, I won't be calling you back to get Haggart."

When Carl cast the warden a quizzical look, Cartwright said, "You know, his grandma died not too long ago. I'm giving him a special pass to spend the weekend with family."

"Guarded?"

"Of course."

When Carl gave the warden a "isn't-that-unusual" look, Warden Cartwright said, "You may leave now, Carl."

Confident the guard was out of earshot and aware his plan was working, Ironman smirked at the warden. "Well…well…well. It's good to see you warden. I hope your family is well." Ironman looked around the warden's office. "Where's my twin?"

Warden Cartwright nodded in the direction of the bathroom.

Ironman sauntered up to the bathroom door and opened it. Seth was standing with his back to the small barred window.

"Well I'll be d___. We do look alike. Kind of. I'm more handsome, of course, but…you'll do."

Seth said nothing. He just stared at Ironman, hoping he didn't see the sweat on his forehead. "Okay…okay… let's get this ball rolling," Ironman said. "Take off your clothes, sweetheart."

Seth did as he was told. Five minutes later, Ironman was dressed in Seth's clothes and Seth in Ironman's orange jumpsuit.

Using duct tape the warden was ordered to bring, Ironman bound Seth hand and foot to the commode and gagged him. He put on Seth's sunglasses and ball cap, and pressing the inside lock button on the bathroom door, he pulled it shut. Ironman then stepped before the warden's desk, gave him a big smile, and said, "Shall we leave warden, sir, or should I say…bro?"

The Warden glared at Ironman but said nothing. Instead, he stood, opened the office door and as soon as Ironman stepped over the threshold, locked it behind them. Five minutes later, he and Ironman pulled alongside the guard house and stopped. To better hide his identity, Ironman had stretched out on the back seat, one arm across his face.

Josh stepped forward. Once again, he peered inside the SUV, first at the warden, then the back seat where Ironman lay. He looked back at the warden. His eyebrows raised in confusion. *Why would the warden's brother still be so wiped out?*

To cover for Ironman, the warden quickly lied. "I'm afraid my brother's got a little upset stomach. He…vomited just a few minutes ago."

Not fully convinced, Josh looked back at Ironman and said, "I hope you get to feeling better soon, sir."

Ironman said nothing. With one arm still covering his face, he raised and lowered the other momentarily to acknowledge that he had heard the guard.

Not completely satisfied, Josh nonetheless stood erect, wrote something on his clipboard, and said to the warden, "Have a good day sir."

CHAPTER 21

Monday afternoon

1:30 p.m.

Jesse and Billy had just finished their lunch at Applebee's and were drinking a second cup of coffee when Billy's cell phone rang. It was the vice warden of Georgia State Prison, Trevor Dunbar. Like Billy, Trevor was a full-blooded Cherokee. Both he and Billy had been raised on the Qualla Boundary, the official name for the reservation owned by the Eastern Band of the Cherokees. Billy and Trevor had gone to school together.

"Billy?"

"Yeah."

"This is Trevor."

"Good to hear from you. It's been a long time."

"I'm not so sure you're going to think it's all that good when you hear what I've got to say."

"Shoot."

"It's Ironman. He's escaped."

Billy paused in disbelief. He palmed the phone and shared the news with Jesse,

then continued his conversation with Trevor. "How'd it happen?"

Trevor shared how Ironman had tricked them. "You know, ever since you and…what's his name? Your brother-in-law…?"

"…Jesse. Jesse Striker. He's here with me as we speak."

"Good. This message is really for both of you. Ironman's never stopped talking about getting even with you guys. I thought you needed a heads up."

"Thanks, man. We appreciate it. If you hear anything else, you let me know…okay?"

"You got it."

*   *   *

With no idea of Ironman's plans or timetable, Billy and Jesse vowed to take no chances. They would immediately head home. Both threw a tip on the table and left Applebee's. "Call me after you get home," Jesse said as he opened the door to his Cobalt and slid inside.

Standing by his Dodge Ram, Billy nodded.

Thirty seconds later, he and Jesse were speeding toward their respective homes, Billy to Gatlinburg and Jesse to Wears Valley.

Billy tried to call Woya on her cell phone but only got her voice mail. Frustrated, he threw his phone on the passenger seat and stepped on the accelerator. It took only thirty minutes for Billy to arrive at his home off Ski Mountain Road. He shifted his Dodge Ram into low and began pulling up the one-hundred foot concrete drive. As it skidded to a stop, he threw open the door, stood and immediately didn't like what he saw.

The front door.

It was wide open.

He hadn't expected Woya, Chloe, or Nathan to be home. One afternoon each week, alternating between their two children, Woya would take Chloe or Nathan to Gatlinburg or Pigeon Forge for an afternoon together. They would shop, have lunch, then see a movie. When it wasn't one of their turns, the other would go with Billy to his office in Gatlinburg.

On this holiday Monday, there was no school, and Nathan was at a birthday party for a friend. And it was Chloe's turn for a mother/daughter outing. Chloe had opted for shopping and Pizza Hut.

The day chosen for Woya's family outings varied. And today, Woya had chosen Monday. When Billy had asked why, she quoted a line from a "Carpenter's" song. It came out as a question: *"Rainy Days and Mondays Always Get Me Down?"*

"Makes sense," Billy said, smiling. "Have a good time."

Not knowing whether Ironman had already left a calling card, Billy was especially thankful Woya had chosen this Monday for her and the kids to be away from home. His only concern was—

The open door.

Being the wife of a PI, one who had made his share of enemies in his fifteen years as a private detective, Woya knew better than to ever leave a door unlocked. Let alone leave one wide open.

Billy gently pressed the car door shut to make as little noise as possible. He pulled his Glock from its holster and crept up the thirty steps that led to the landing and the front door. He slipped to one side, raised his pistol to his right ear, and listened intently for any sound from within.

Hearing none, he stepped through the open door. He held his breath as his eyes panned the living room and the kitchen.

No one.

He then softly padded down the hall. One after another, he stood with his back to the side of each of three bedroom doors before entering.

There was no one in the house. Billy sighed and lowered his pistol to his side. He then stepped back into the living room.

That's when he noticed it. Above the fireplace, painted in blood red letters was the word…OREMUNER.

What the h___?

Not knowing what to think, Billy sat on the couch and called Jesse.

CHAPTER 22

When Jesse arrived home, everything seemed okay. Melissa and Abigail weren't there, but he hadn't expected them to be. Every Monday, Wednesday, and Friday afternoon, they went to the "Y."

But something wasn't right. It was a feeling, but— more than that.

Jesse slipped out of his Cobalt. He stepped onto the front porch and immediately, his eyes were drawn to a word smeared on the door. It was slathered in large, red letters. *Blood?* He'd never seen or heard of such a word. *OREMUNER?*

That's when Jesse heard a gurgling sound. It had come from the other side of the porch. He immediately knew what it was, what it had to be—

BABE!

Babe was Abigail's three year old Yorkshire Terrier.

Jesse bounded down the steps, raced to the far side of the porch and there, lying on her side was Babe. Her throat had been slit. It was Babe's blood on the door.

Tears, born of sadness and anger erupted as Jesse knelt beside Babe.

Just then, his cell phone rang. It was Billy. While Jesse tried to compose himself, Billy shared what had happened when he arrived home. Jesse did the same. "Man, I'm sorry about Babe." There was a brief moment of silence, then Billy said, "Any idea of what OREMUNER means?"

"Not a clue," Jesse said, standing.

After a brief pause, Billy suggested they get together at Jesse's and discuss how to deal with Ironman.

"You name the time," Jesse said.

"7:00?"

"Works for me."

"In the meantime, I'm going to call Bud and let him know what's happening."

Bud was Bud Bradley, Chief of Police of the Gatlinburg Police Department. He picked up on the second ring. In the minutes that followed, Billy filled him in on Ironman's escape and what he, Jesse, and their families had been experiencing. He also asked him about the word OREMUNER. "Mean anything to you?"

"Doesn't even sound like a word."

Bradley promised to have his officers make periodic drive-bys of their homes. Billy then called FBI Bureau Chief , Harrelson. He promised Billy he and his agents would be on the lookout for Ironman.

For further protection, Jesse called several friends from the Do Jo where he worked out—black belts, current and ex-police, retired special ops soldiers, and others who willingly agreed to guard their homes on a rotating basis.

* * *

It was a little past 7:00 when Billy, Woya, Chloe, and Nathan arrived at the Striker's. Chloe, Nathan, and Abigail went to the front yard to play.

"I'm sorry about Babe," Chloe said to Abigail.

"Thanks." Looking close to tears, Abigail said, "Do you think dogs go to heaven?"

"Dad says they do. He says it's an Indian belief that all living things are children of the earth, whether they have feet or wings or roots."

"I hope so."

The children then began playing "Red Light, Green Light" while the adults sat on the back porch discussing, among other things, what the word OREMUNER might mean.

"It's got to be some other language," Jesse said. "Or… maybe it's a code word for…who knows what."

Following a brief pause, Jesse said. "I have an idea. I think we should contact an etymologist at the university."

"A what?" Billy said.

"An etymologist. You didn't learn that in PI school?" Jesse raised his eyebrows in faux surprise, then confessed, "I wouldn't have known that word either had I not used it in a novel. An etymologist, my friend, is one who studies etymology."

"Well, that helps. Thanks, Jesse."

Enjoying the stress-relieving banter, Jesse smiled once again. "Etymology. E-T-Y-M-O-L-O-G-Y. It's the study of the history of words.

"And you think there's an etymologist at UTK?" Billy asked.

"Don't know. But I suspect someone in their English Department would have some expertise when it comes to our mystery word. I think we should make an appointment.

"Do it."

CHAPTER 23

Doctor Hugh Warren was the head of UTK's English Department. The earliest he could meet with Jesse and Billy was Wednesday at 10:00 a.m. It was 9:50 when Billy pulled his Dodge Ram beneath McClaren Tower and parked. He and Jesse got out and took the elevator to the fifth floor.

"Doctor Warren," Jesse said as he and Billy entered. "I appreciate you taking time to see us." Turning to Billy he said, "This is my good friend, Billy Whitecloud."

"Nice to meet both of you," Professor Warren said. Then to Jesse he added, "You're the author…right?"

"Yes, sir."

"I've heard good things about your writing, Mr. Striker."

"Thanks. And please call me, Jesse."

"Jesse. Like I said, I've heard good things about your writing. The last book, what was it…?"

"Angel…"

"Yes…that's it. It was a best seller, I believe."

"Yes, it was. I'm grateful."

"Well, in all honesty, I haven't read any of your novels. I pretty much stick to the classics. But…I've heard a lot about them from my students."

Jesse had gotten used to literary academia's distain for popular fiction. That the professor even knew he was an author was nothing short of amazing.

Doctor Warren reached out his hand to shake Jesse's, then Billy's, while attempting to rise from his chair. Unfortunately, when it seemed to rise with him, he gave up. By all appearances, the good doctor was not a man who had done a lot of exercise over his fifty-five years. Whatever upper body muscle he may have had had long since gone. From the chest on down, he resembled a pear.

"Have a seat, gentlemen."

Jesse again thanked the professor as he and Billy sat on two black, faux leather chairs before the professor's oak desk. At five-nine, Jesse felt it necessary to sit up straight to see over the mounds of books, papers, and memorabilia that cluttered Doctor Warren's desk.

"Well, I did some research on the mystery word you sent me. OREMUNER? Correct?"

"That's right," Billy said.

"O-R-E-M-U-N-E-R?"

"Yes."

"It didn't take long to discover that…there is no such word."

"What do you mean, doctor?"

"I mean OREMUNER is most likely a coded word of some sort.

"Exactly what do you mean by a coded word?" Jesse asked.

"I mean, whoever spray-painted that word on the wall and door of your homes…"

"…I'm afraid it wasn't spray paint, doctor. It was blood."

"Oh, my goodness!"

A few seconds slipped by as the doctor internalized that reality. Jesse brought him back to the subject at hand. "So…what do you mean when you say our word might be a coded word?"

"It's been altered. Provided it's a real word, in some language, known or unknown, the letters have been jumbled up in some way. Fortunately, whoever put that word on your wall and door made the simplest of codes. He just wrote the letters backwards. In other words, OREMUNER is actually RENUMERO.

"By the sound of it, I immediately knew it was some form of Latin. After a little checking, I discovered that RENUMERO is Latin for…PAY BACK. Does that make any sense to either of you?"

Billy and Jesse exchanged glances, then Billy said, "It most certainly does, Doctor. Thanks. You've been a great help."

CHAPTER 24

Saturday.

8:00 p.m.

"What does one wear?"

Ever since Jesse had asked, Masumi had had second thoughts about attending church with Jesse and Melissa. But she had promised, and there was no getting out of it. Certainly not the evening before.

She couldn't remember having ever been in church. She had. Surely. Maybe as a child, but those memories had long ago been sealed away in her subconscious. In any case, she didn't have the slightest idea of what today's church-goers wore. So—she called Jesse and asked to speak to Melissa.

"Wear anything you like, Masumi. Really. Some people dress up; some come in jeans. Nobody cares."

"What if I just wear what I wear to work?"

"That would be fine. Just…be comfortable."

"Okay. Okay. I can do that."

*   *   *

Sunday morning.

Jesse, Melissa, and Abigail picked up Masumi at 9:00. Worship was at 10:00 and, depending on the Sunday morning traffic in Knoxville, they would arrive ten to fifteen minutes before the service.

Masumi was wearing a casual, abstract pintuck blouse. It was holly berry and black in color and had a mandarin collar and long sleeves. Her knee length skirt was black.

"You look great," Melissa said as Masumi slipped into the back seat beside Abigail. "But…like I said, you could have come in a gunnysack and no one would care."

Twenty-five minutes of small talk later, Jesse pulled the Cobalt onto the Fellowship parking lot."

"Wow!" Masumi said. "I can't believe how big your church is."

And Fellowship was big. The building sat on a seven acre plot of ground and was surrounded by a blacktop parking lot.

"How many people worship here?"

"Total?" Jesse said. "About six thousand. Not in every service. On any given Sunday, there are probably a thousand or more in each of three worship services."

Masumi shook her head in surprise. In Berkley, where she had lived most of her adult life, no one went to church, or at least, that's what it seemed. And, in her mind, certainly not thousands of people."

As they entered, Masumi was surprised to see there were no pews. Instead, the entire worship area was filled with theater seats that descended downward toward a raised stage.

On the stage was a ten member praise worship team. They had already begun singing as she and the Strikers took their seats near the front of the middle section. Once seated, Masumi raised her eyebrows in surprise. The music was not what she had expected. It was contemporary, and the praise team was good. Really good.

Masumi looked before her and to her left and right. She quickly turned around and glanced at the hundreds of worshipers behind her. She turned back as the pastor stepped up to the front of the raised stage and addressed the worshipers.

Masumi glanced at her bulletin to see who he was. His name was Carter. Dr. Noah Carter. He appeared to be in his late thirties or early forties.

As was his custom, he greeted the congregation, gave a special welcome to visitors, and then led them in a prayer. He then asked them to "Share the Peace," which at Fellowship, was an invitation to greet one another.

Two minutes later, Pastor Carter asked for everyone to be seated. He then paused. His eyes panned the worshipers and a hush of expectation settled over them. And then, he spoke.

His message for the day, like every Sunday, was expository. It was based on a text of Scripture. Today the text was 2 Corinthians, Chapter 6, verse 2. He read it: *"Now is the time of God's favor. Now is the day of salvation."*

Pastor Carter explained the text for the day, peppering it with clarifying comments and a few appropriate real life illustrations that made the text come alive. They were never personal in nature, until—today.

CHAPTER 25

Toward the end of his message and prior to his invitation, Pastor Carter said, "I want to tell you something I have never told anyone. And I can assure you I have never mentioned it in a sermon. Certainly not here, or in the two other congregations I have served."

Pastor Carter paused. As in the beginning, his eyes panned the crowd below, and then those in the balcony. Gradually, a hush fell on the worshipers.

It lasted no more than ten seconds, but it seemed much longer. Some probably thought the pastor forgot what he was going to say. The reality was, what he was about to share was of such a personal nature that he knew that some would be shocked. When finally his eyes returned to the worshipers below, he said, "I want you to know something about me…I am an alcoholic."

The quietness that always accompanied the pastor's sermons, deepened. It was followed by a hint of murmuring. It ended when Pastor Carter continued.

"I began drinking seriously when I was twenty-five. I wasn't a Christian at the time. And it got worse. A lot worse when I was faced with something I just couldn't handle. My wife and I were driving home from a local blues bar. It was a Saturday night. It was dark. And rainy. I think it was about 1:00 a.m.

"We picked up our daughter, Emma, at the babysitter's. I noticed that our sitter, Amanda, had a concerned look on her face. She probably smelled my breath.

"The truth is, I had one too many drinks. No, make that *many* too many drinks before I drove my lovely wife Sarah and our two year daughter home. She was in the back, in her car seat. But…we never made it home."

Pastor Carter paused. He did something Jesse and Melissa had never seen him do. He pulled a handkerchief from his hip pocket and wiped his eyes. Suddenly, the song, "The Sound of Silence" took on new meaning as the proverbial "You could hear a pin drop" cliché became a reality at Fellowship Church.

Pastor Carter continued, "We were on a two lane road. All I can remember is weaving across the center line, into the path of an oncoming vehicle. I was later told it was a semi. Its lights blurred in front of me. Its air horn was blaring. And…I heard my wife screaming, that and the sound of crunching metal and cracking glass. And then…everything went black.

"I lay in a coma for two months. When I awoke, I was told that my wife and my beautiful daughter had been killed instantly. That's when I went from a heavy drinker to an alcoholic. I became…a drunk.

"For two years, I drank myself into unconsciousness. I woke up in places I'd never been before. Sometimes with someone I had never seen before. Sometimes in a park, sometimes under an overpass, sometimes …I don't know where.

"Then one evening, a group of Christians came to the underpass where I and several others lay, some asleep, some still drinking, some begging for a drink from a fellow who had a nearly full bottle of cheap wine.

"These Christians handed out brochures. They spoke of a Franklin Graham revival. It was scheduled for the next day. They offered to come, to give any who were willing, a ride.

"Well, I did my best to sober up, pulled what I hoped to be a somewhat clean shirt and jeans from my knapsack, and accepted their ride. Graham was preaching at Neyland Stadium on the campus of the University of Tennessee in Knoxville. It was packed. I didn't know then but, there were over 100 thousand people there.

"I don't remember exactly what Franklin Graham preached that day. What I do know is that, when he called those who wanted to receive Jesus Christ as Lord and Savior to come to the front, I couldn't get there fast enough.

"I haven't had a drink since. A year of sobriety later, I attended seminary. Four years after that, I was ordained into the ministry. I was thirty-two. That was ten years ago.

"Now, why have I told you this story? Just this, in this fallen world, bad things happen. Sometimes they're no fault of our own; sometimes they are, as was certainly true in my case.

"I know this, all of you have experienced tough times, some tougher than others. There are people here who have lost jobs. You don't know how you are going to make ends meet. Some of you have experienced a death in your families. Some of you are ill. Maybe it's heart disease. Maybe…cancer.

"Worse, some of you here today don't personally know Jesus Christ. I want you to know that He is the solution to every problem we face. He, and He alone, can give you peace. He came to this earth for that very purpose. He came to die on a cross to pay for your sins and mine. And, He promised that all who believe that and trust in Him, would receive not only peace, but forgiveness of sins and the promise of heaven.

"If you have not received Jesus Christ, now is the time to receive Him. Now is the day of salvation."

In the brief moment of silence that followed, the pianist played softly in the background while the praise team slipped up behind Pastor Carter. And then they began singing, "Come Just As You Are." Everyone joined in. Following the last stanza, the praise team began to hum and Pastor Carter once again spoke: "If God is speaking to your heart, I want you to…come, just as you are." The pastor then folded his hands in prayer and raised them to the chin of his bowed head.

Masumi's tears began to flow. Melissa glanced in her direction. Her eyes welled up as well as she put her arm around Masumi.

Much later, on the ride back to her apartment, they rode in silence. When they arrived, Masumi opened the back seat car door and started to get out, and then stopped. She turned around and said, "Thanks. I want you to know that I was really moved. I…I want to believe, I really do."

"Masumi," Jesse said. We'll be praying for you, okay? And let me give you a promise, if you truly *want* to believe, in time…you will. I don't know when, but believe me…it will happen."

CHAPTER 26

Tuesday.

10:50 a.m.

"Where's Dad?" Chloe asked as she came in from outside. She was spattered with blue paint. Her dad had made her day when he suggested she and Nathan paint the old shed in the woods behind their chalet.

"He's with Uncle Jesse," Woya said, adding, "Did you get any paint on the shed?"

"A little." Chloe giggled. "Wait till you see Nathan."

Suddenly, Woya and Chloe heard a loud rumbling. It was an all too familiar sound in Gatlinburg. It was the sound of Harleys. It had come from Ski Mountain Road. Judging from the gradual increase in decibels, one or more Harleys were coming up their drive.

"MOM!" Nathan yelled as he barged through the screen door. He turned toward his mother, than stared back out the front door. "Someone's coming up the drive. There are two motorcycles and a big black van."

Even if Nathan hadn't warned her, Woya knew who it was. Who it had to be. Ironman or a couple of his goons.

"GET INTO YOUR BEDROOMS. FAST. AND LOCK THE DOORS!"

"Why?" Chloe asked.

"JUST DO IT!" Woya shouted.

As soon as they were out of sight, she turned, stepped through the screen door and onto the front porch. Two men dressed in black from head to toe had just shut off their engines. A third got out of the van. All three were walking up the thirty steps to the porch. She could smell the exhaust from their cycles as it wafted on a light breeze.

"What do you want?" Woya asked, glaring at the men as they reached the porch and stopped.

"In a word?" said one. "You. Get your kids. We're going for a ride." He had a Spanish accent.

"We're not going anywhere with you," Woya said, and spinning around, she raced into the first floor bedroom, yanked open the drawer to the end table, and pulled out Billy's backup Glock. The men were right behind her.

As she spun around, one of them, the one with the Spanish accent, grabbed her wrist, twisted it, and yanked the pistol from her hand.

"Like I said, get your kids." When Woya just stood there, he yelled, "NOW!"

* * *

"Where are you taking us?" Woya asked as the two bikers dragged her, Chloe and Nathan down the steps to the awaiting van and shoved them inside. No one answered.

Once in the van, she asked again. "Where are you taking us?"

This time, she directed her question to a third biker who had presumably been in the back of the van from the start. He had an unkempt beard and hair that was long, black, and stringy, like it hadn't been washed in a couple weeks. Or more. Like the other two bikers, he said nothing. He just cocked his head to one side and flashed her a wicked, spaced-out grin.

Woya then glanced at the rear view mirror and gasped when she saw the driver. He had the most evil eyes, and he was glaring at her. That's when she knew who he was…who he had to be.

"You're Ironman, aren't you?"

He didn't answer. He just slowly turned his head to the front, started the van, and began to descend the steep drive to Ski Mountain Road.

"Who's Ironman, Mom?" Chloe whispered.

To protect their children, Billy and Woya had agreed to say nothing about Billy's involvement in Ironman's capture or about his escape. Woya didn't answer. She just shook her head and tried to focus on where they were being taken.

She had a pretty good idea. Woya knew Gatlinburg well enough to know that they were heading toward Pigeon Forge. Ten minutes later, when they made a left, she was sure they had turned on 321. That was the road to Wears Valley and Jesse and Melissa's cabin.

From Pigeon Forge, Woya knew it took about seventeen minutes to get there. It seemed that maybe they had been on the road that long when the van slowed and turned left. That had to be Bryan Street.

Up ahead, about a quarter of a mile, there was a stop sign at the corner of Linden and Walker. The van stopped, then turned right. Another quarter of a mile later and the van took another right. Surely, that was Marshall Lane. If so, they were now less than three minutes from Jesse and Melissa's log cabin. When the van began ascending the steep drive and stopped, Woya had no doubt where they were. They were at the Strikers'.

Ironman rolled down the window, and shouted, "Bring em' in."

Woya couldn't see who he had spoken to, but when the side door of the van slid open, she knew that two more bikers had come to the Strikers' and kidnapped Melissa and Abigail.

"O my God," Melissa said when she saw Woya, Chloe and Nathan. Before Woya could respond, Melissa was pushed from behind. She stumbled into the van, followed by Abigail.

"Where are they taking us?" Melissa asked.

Woya just shrugged her shoulders.

"Bag 'em," Ironman said to his accomplice, who obediently slipped a black hood over Melissa, Abigail, Woya, and her kids.

CHAPTER 27

Tuesday.

12:00 p.m.

"I can't believe Ironman escaped."

The one speaking was Ted Parker. He was a retired Navy Seal and a good friend of Jesse and Billy. He was driving his burgundy Jeep Cherokee. Wes Baker was in the passenger seat.

Ted had just turned up the steep drive to the Striker's cabin. Both he and Wes had gladly agreed to be a part of a rotating group of guys who would keep a close watch on Jesse and Billy's homes.

"Yeah. Just glad we could help out," Wes said.

A fellow Tae Kwon Do black belt, Wes was a good friend of Jesse's. Both worked out at the same dojo in Knoxville.

When Ted turned off the engine, he looked in silence at the front door. It was wide open. "This doesn't look good," he said as he opened the car door, stepped out and walked up the steps to the front porch. Baker was close behind.

They stopped on either side of the door. "MELISSA? ABIGAIL?" Wes shouted.

There was no response.

Ted and Wes glanced at one another. Ted then silently nodded his head toward the open doorway, stepped inside, and once again yelled, "MELISSA? ABIGAIL?"

Hearing no response, they walked throughout the cabin in silence. "I don't like this," Ted said as he pulled his cell phone from his front jeans pocket and poked in Jesse's number.

Seconds later, Jesse got on the line."

"Jesse, this is Ted. Wes is with me."

"What's up?"

"You sittin' down?"

"Yeah. Billy and I are at Hardee's having lunch. Why?"

"Were Melissa and Abigail going anywhere this morning?"

"No…I specifically told them to wait for you guys."

There was an uncomfortable silence on the line.

"Is something wrong?" Jesse asked.

Ted looked at Wes with raised eyebrows. "Jesse… they're not here."

"WHAT? ARE YOU SURE?"

"I'm afraid so."

"WHAT ABOUT BILLY'S FAMILY?"

"Jesse, I…don't know."

"Do you know who was going there?"

"Yeah. Sure. We met at a McDonalds for lunch before leaving. Jim and Pete."

"You got their number?"

"Yeah."

"Call them."

Ted did, and a minute later, he called Jesse.

"Jesse?"

"Yeah?"

"I'm sorry. But…Woya and the kids are not there."

Jesse hung up. He shared what had happened with Billy. Anger and fear converged within him. And to avoid bashing his fist on the table, he closed his eyes, looked upward, and drew in a deep breath. He let it out, pulled his cell phone from his belt clip, and punched in the Knoxville FBI director's number.

"Who are you calling?"

"Harrelson."

* * *

As they drove along, Melissa listened intently to their surroundings. At first, there was the whirr of rubber on blacktop. Judging from the constant stream of cars and semi's, it was most likely an interstate. Probably 75.

A little over four hours later, the interstate gave way to the gritty sound of crushed rock as the van began an upward, twisting climb on an uneven rutted road.

A logging road?

Occasionally, Melissa could hear the gurgling of river water that flowed first on one side, then the other. Periodically, it was drowned out by the sound of Harleys. Clearly, they were following behind the van.

Melissa guessed that maybe a half-hour had passed when the van and the motorcycles stopped. As the Harleys continued to idle, Melissa heard the click of the driver's side door as it opened and Ironman got out. The ex-con who had ridden with them, slid open the side door, and said, "STAY PUT!" He joined Ironman.

To the bikers, Ironman said, "You guys go on ahead."

Melissa had no idea what that meant. But soon, four Harleys, one after another, rumbled past the van. Their collective, stuttering growl, gradually faded, then gave way to the silence of the woods. It was accompanied by the sound of footsteps outside the van.

"Okay, ladies and kiddies." It was Ironman. "Time for us to take a little hike." The ex-con who had ridden with them, whom they would later learn went by the biker name, "Smoky," removed their hoods. He untied their hands and said, "GET OUT!"

Woya stepped out first, then Chloe, her arms tightly clutching her mother's waist. Melissa and Abigail were next. Only little Nathan remained in the van. He stood before the open side door. His hands were balled into tiny fists and his lips were squeezed tightly as he glared at Ironman.

Ironman just smiled. He then thrust his hands beneath Nathan's arms, hoisted him out of the van, and set him on the ground. And leaning within inches of Nathan's face, he said, "Well, aren't you the tough one, little man."

Ironman then straightened up and turned his attention to Woya and Melissa. "Okay, this is what we're going to do. We're going to take us a little walk through the woods. About a mile in all. It'll take us to a cabin where I'm going to allow you to stay...rent free."

The ex-con who had ridden with them belched out a laugh.

"No...no...ladies...and kiddies, don't you go and thank me."

He then spoke to Smoky, "You take the lead, and I'll follow behind our guests."

CHAPTER 28

The four ex-cons had just reached the end of the narrow path. It opened into a clearing, from where one could see the cabin one hundred yards away. Stick, so named because he was beanpole thin, was in the lead. Suddenly, he hit the brakes. "WHAT THE H___?"

The bikers behind him slid to a stop.

"What is it?" asked the one in the back.

"BEARS!"

A protective mother bear and three cubs had just crossed about thirty feet in front of Stick. It stopped, faced him, rose on its hind legs, and began to growl.

"GUYS…YOU BEST MAKE A LOT OF NOISE OR WE'RE GOING TO BE LUNCH!"

The four ex-cons revved their engines and began to yell. Confused by the sound, the bear turned and began to lumber into the clearing, her three cubs struggling to keep up.

They bounded to the far side of the cabin and through the open door of a weathered barn, a couple hundred feet away.

"Well, that was close," Stick said as he motioned for the others to follow him to the cabin. Three minutes later, they pulled in front and shut off their engines.

Jesse's cabin.

12:40 p.m.

Agent Harrelson, whom many believed could double for the late TV crime boss, Tony Soprano, was standing with his hands on his hips on the front porch of Jesse's cabin when Jesse and Billy pulled up. Ted was sitting on a rocker; Wes was on the porch swing. When they saw Billy and Jesse, they stood. Wes walked to the railing as Jesse ascended the steps. Billy was close behind.

"Sorry, man," Wes said.

"Not your fault," Jesse said.

To his close friend, Agent Harrelson, Billy said. "Thanks for coming, Larry." They shook hands. "Did you find anything?"

"Well, it's a little early. We haven't been here all that long," Harrelson said, motioning for them to follow him inside where two Knoxville Police Officers, assisting the FBI, were dusting for prints. "So far, it looks like we've already found a few prints. Of course, you know how it works. Most are Jesse's and his family."

Glancing at Billy, he added, "We'll probably find yours and Woya's in here as well…and all the kids. That said, if Ironman was in here or any of his goons, and if they touched anything, we'll eventually have their prints.

"In one sense though, it may not make a lot of difference. Judging from the tire tracks outside, there were definitely a couple of motorcycles here, maybe more. And some make or model of a truck or van. I don't think there's any doubt that it was Ironman who…"

Harrelson hesitated, not wanting to mention the obvious.

"…Kidnapped our families?" Jesse said.

"That would be my guess."

"What about Billy's home?" Jesse asked.

"Agents Peterson and McGill are there. Looks about the same. Motorcycles. A truck or van. We may know more when we look at the prints. But, then again, maybe not."

Jesse gritted his teeth and walked toward the open front door. He stood on the threshold for a moment, then turning back toward Harrelson, he said, "What do we do now?"

"Well, you and Billy need to be here at all times in case Ironman calls."

"Shouldn't someone be at *my* home?" Billy asked.

"Maybe just to make sure no one breaks in. A volunteer or two could take care of that."

"What if Ironman calls my home?" Billy said.

"We'll have our guys here, at Jesse's, 24/7 and channel all calls here, including any that would come to your home."

When Billy seemed satisfied with the plan, Harrelson continued, "Hopefully, when Ironman calls, we can triangulate it and find out where they're keeping your families."

About a half hour later, Harrelson and the officers assisting the FBI left.

"Why don't we stick together," Jesse said to Billy. "When we're here, Ted and Wes can leave and Jim and Pete can watch your home. If they can't stay…" Jesse looked at Ted and Wes, "…maybe you guys can stay there?"

Ted and Wes looked at one another and nodded. "Of course," Ted said. "I'm coordinating the whole thing. We can have someone at either location, any time, day or night. Just keep us posted where you guys are. Okay?"

"You got it," Billy said.

"Thanks guys," Jesse said to Ted and Wes. Then to Billy he said, "So, you're okay with us sticking together for now?"

"Sure. That's probably best." Looking at Ted, then Wes, Billy said, "I guess you two can take off for now. If you don't mind, call Jim and Pete and make sure at least one of them stays at my home."

Ted and Wes agreed, then left. Billy and Jesse followed them out the door and stood alone on the porch. "What now?" Jesse asked Billy.

"I can think of only one thing."

"Which is?"

"Let's pray."

CHAPTER 29

It was 4:30 when Smoky led the Whiteclouds and Strikers into the clearing, followed by Ironman. It didn't take Melissa long to realize why Smoky had been given that biker name. During their half hour walk through the woods, not a moment passed when he wasn't smoking something. Sometimes it had a sweet smell, sometimes it didn't.

As they reached the steps to the front porch, Ironman took charge. "Stay here," he said. He ascended the steps, opened the screen door, and stood inside. His eyes panned the living room.

Bear was lounging in a faded, frayed La-Z-Boy, his back to Ironman. His eyes were locked on the Cartwrights who were seated on the couch. When he heard Ironman enter, he spun around in the swivel chair and said, "Hey man, good to see you."

Ironman said nothing. He just looked past Bear at three Georgia Ex-Cons who were sitting at the kitchen counter, their backs to him. They were laughing about something one of them had said. Upon hearing Bear's greeting, they immediately stopped and turned their heads toward Ironman.

In the silence that followed, Ironman walked through the back door and onto the porch where four other bikers were bantering about something. It ceased the moment Ironman stepped onto the porch.

"Everything okay, Boss?" Snake asked.

Once again, Ironman said nothing. He just nodded, turned, and walked back into the living room. He stepped up to the five Cartwrights. "You're going to have some company," he said. Then slowly wheeling about, he walked back to the front porch. As he stepped near the threshold, he felt something.

A presence.

He had never felt anything like it before. It was like stepping into an unseen electrical field. What he couldn't see, or know, was that Adryel was standing beside him, looking down on him, and—he wasn't smiling.

Ironman was then struck with another sensation. One new to him. Fear. It wasn't much, but it was enough to be upsetting. He gazed upward to his right. Like staring into a one way mirror but seeing no one, Ironman had no way of knowing he was looking directly into Adryel's eyes.

"Something wrong, Boss?" Smoky asked.

Thankful for the distraction, Ironman looked down at him, shook his head to free himself of the unseen apparition and said, "No…no…nothing's wrong."

He then looked at the Whiteclouds and the Strikers and said, "You guys come on in. I want you to meet some of our other guests."

Fearing what lay ahead, Woya, Melissa and the kids stood frozen in their tracks.

"NOW!" Ironman shouted, motioning toward the open door with his head.

In the hours that followed, the Whiteclouds and Strikers became acquainted with the Cartwrights. An unseen bond formed among them. It was like the one felt by prisoners who shared a common enemy.

Ironman gave Woya , Melissa, and Abigail the same instructions he had given to Roland's family and to Andrea and Madison. He then turned and headed for the back porch. When he was gone, Woya looked at the Cartwrights and said, "Would you like to pray?"

The Cartwrights exchanged glances but said nothing. You would have thought Woya had been them if they wanted to take a walk on hot coals.

But given their present situation, they gave in. Praying had to be better than nothing, right?

Woya, Chloe, Nathan, Melissa, and Abigail held hands. Little Nathan and Abigail, who stood at each end, reached out their hands to the Cartwrights nearest them. Not knowing what else to do, they also stood and joined hands with their new acquaintances as Woya led them all in prayer.

CHAPTER 30

Early Wednesday
2:30 a.m.

Light from the full moon filtered through the living room window. It fell on Tall Man, casting a long shadow over twelve-year-old Madison as she lay fast asleep, huddled on one corner of the couch.

Outside, crickets were scratching out their telepathic messages while inside, the sound of snoring pricked the silence. Occasionally, there was the rattling of loose fitted windows as the wind periodically gusted.

Tall Man towered over Madison. He then looked about the living room. As best he could tell, everyone was fast asleep. His confidence bolstered, he bent forward and gently poked Madison on the shoulder. She jerked awake and stared wide-eyed at Tall Man. He quickly put a finger to his lips and said, "...Schhhhh…"

As Tall Man had done, Madison looked about the room to see if anyone else was awake. Seeing no one, she whispered, "What do you want?"

"I want to help you," he whispered. "You need to slowly and quietly get up and follow me."

"What about my Mom, and the others?"

Tall Man rose to his full height of six-seven. He glanced about the room for a second time to make sure no one was listening. He then leaned close to Madison and again whispered, "I'm going to come back and free them as well. Later. Okay?" Tall Man then reached out his hand to Madison. Still wary, she hesitated, then slowly took it.

Once again, Tall Man put his finger vertically across his lips as he led Madison through the maze of bodies, careful not to step on anyone. A few seconds later, he and Madison were on the back porch.

Suddenly—

Someone on the porch, hidden in the darkness, snored. It had come from the swing. One of the ex-cons lay on it in a near fetal position. It was Slow Beef. As Tall Man slipped by him with Madison in tow, a loose board creaked. It awakened Slow Beef.

"Hey," he said. "Where you going?"

"None of your d___ business. Go back to sleep."

Slow Beef smiled, nodded in agreement and closed his eyes and, seconds later, was again snoring. Tall Man then tightened his grip on Madison's hand and led her off the back porch.

"You're hurting me!"

"Get used to it," he said as he dragged Madison toward the open door of the barn. "It ain't nothing compared to the hurt I'm about to give you, sweetheart."

Less than a minute later, as Tall Man attempted to step through the open barn door, he smacked in to something like—like an unseen wall. But it wasn't a wall. It was Adryel, blocking the way inside the barn.

Aware of Tall Man's lecherous intentions, Adryel struck an unseen blow to Tall Man's face, causing him to let go of Madison and throw his hands to his busted nose. He thumped to the ground, seat first. Perplexed and frightened by his invisible assailant, he shouted, "WHAT THE H___!"

Freed from his grip, Madison screamed, spun around, and raced for the cabin as Adryel picked Tall Man up and raised him off the ground. With powerful unseen arms, Adryel thrust him against the side of the barn. He hit with a thud and instantly slid to the ground, unconscious.

CHAPTER 31

Awakened by her screams, Slow Beef awoke with a start. He sat up on the swing and cast a confused look at Madison as she bounded up the two porch steps and raced for the back door. "What's wrong, little girl," he said, reaching out a thick arm to block her.

"LET GO OF ME!" she screamed.

"I don't mean you no harm," he said as he released her.

Madison banged through the screen door amidst the mutterings and curses of ex-cons rudely rousted from their sleep.

"MOMMY!"

Madison stepped on one of the ex-cons huddled on the floor near the couch. "HEY, WHAT THE H___'s GOIN' ON!"

Suddenly, the lights flicked on. Ironman was standing at the foot of the loft stairs. He slowly walked up to Madison who was now safely tucked in her mother's arms. He stood over both. "What's the matter, girl?"

Madison, who was still sobbing, relayed what had happened.

Had there been more light in the room, everyone would have seen Ironman's face turn red. He spun around, marched out the back door and onto the porch.

"Hey boss," Slow Beef said.

Ironman stopped in front of the swing. "What in the h___'s goin' on?"

"I think Tall Man done something to that little girl."

"Where is he?"

Slow Beef pointed toward the barn.

As Ironman marched off the porch and headed for the barn, several ex-cons gathered and leaned on the railing.

Ironman slowed as he saw Tall Man, leaning against the barn near the open door. He was just beginning to come to when Ironman towered over him.

"WHAT DID YOU DO TO THAT LITTLE GIRL?"

"I didn't do nothing."

"Really? It's bad enough if you tried something, but it'll only be worse if you lie to me."

"Okay…okay. No big deal. I was just going to have a little fun with her, you know." Tall Man had a smile on his face, one that suddenly disappeared when it was met with the toe of Ironman's boot. Teeth cracked and blood spurted from his already smashed nose.

Ironman spun around and marched back to the cabin, past the eleven ex-cons who were now on the back porch. They looked at him as he swept by but said nothing.

135

When Ironman was out of sight and hearing, Snake looked at the others and said, "Who's missing?"

They soon discovered it was Tall Man.

Snake looked at Sanchez. "Maybe you better check on him."

"I will," Sanchez said. But, instead of heading for the barn, he turned and walked inside the cabin, in search of Ironman.

He found him on the front porch, alone, smoking a cigarette. "What do you want me to do with Tall Man?"

Ironman, who was leaning forward on the railing, looked straight ahead and said, "Nothing."

"What do you mean…nothing?"

"You can check on him. That's fine. But when he wakes up, you tell him, he can spend the rest of the night in the barn."

"Gotcha."

*   *   *

3:15 a.m.

"HEY…IT'S COLD OUT HERE!" The slurred voice came from the barn. It was Tall Man. Every five minutes or so, his pained voice, dimmed by distance, reached the back porch. And every time, it was ignored.

Until roughly 4:05 a.m.

This time, it was a scream. Loud. Long. Continuous, and then—it stopped.

*   *   *

6:30 a.m.

Snake, Stick, and Slow Beef were all on the back porch. Each had a cup of coffee in his hand as they waited for breakfast. Snake and Stick were leaning on the railing, staring at the barn.

"Can you see Tall Man?" Snake asked.

"Nope," Stick said.

"Maybe he's not okay."

"Maybe he's just asleep."

To Slow Beef, who was now sitting on the swing, Bear said, "Slow Beef, go check on Tall Man."

Pleased to be trusted to do anything, Slow Beef jumped up out of the swing and began plodding toward the barn. A minute later, he disappeared inside but, only for a few seconds.

"OH MY GOD...OH MY GOD," he shouted as he came lumbering out of the barn as fast as his 280 pounds would allow. He was shaking his head as he stopped before the back porch steps, leaned way forward with his hands on his knees, and gasped for breath.

"What is it, man?" asked Snake.

"It's...it's...Tall Man. He's...all torn up. I think...I think maybe a bear got 'im."

Slow Beef then stood. His usual, pudgy red face was two shades lighter. He squeezed his lips together in a vain effort to stop the eruption. And then, spinning around,

137

he stumbled over to the side of the lot, bent over, and vomited.

When Snake and Stick relayed what had happened to Ironman, his only response was, "Bury him."

CHAPTER 32

Later Wednesday morning.

9:00 a.m.

It was a crisp, forty-eight degrees in Wears Valley. Jesse and Billy were on the front porch of Jesse's cabin. Their breakfast over, they sat in silence on the twin rockers, each lost in his own thoughts and fears over what was happening to their families.

Pointing to Billy's coffee cup, Jesse said, "More?"

Billy nodded.

Jesse walked to the kitchen, picked up a carafe and returned to the porch. He filled Billy's cup, then his. As steam rose from both, he set the carafe on the rustic end table that separated the rockers and sat.

Suddenly—Jesse's cell phone rang.

Wired like an E-string wound one too many times, Jesse flinched. His head snapped toward Billy. For a split second, each held their breath and stared at one another.

The phone rang a second time. Jesse jumped out of the rocker, banged through the screen door and ran to the kitchen counter. He grabbed his cell phone. "WHO IS THIS?"

A moment of excruciating silence followed, and then that unmistakable voice.

"Your worst nightmare."

It was Ironman.

"If you hurt my family, or Billy's, I swear…"

"…Shut the h___ up. You'd think you're in control of this situation."

In the pulsating stillness that followed, Billy entered the living room. He was standing at attention a few feet from Jesse. To confirm what he expected, Jesse silently mouthed Ironman's name and Billy nodded.

Jesse then broke the silence, "How do we get our families back?"

"Well, let's just say, we make an exchange, you two for your families."

"Okay. Okay, so what do you want us to do?"

"You know the old Higgins factory?"

"Of course."

The Higgins factory was a once prosperous, now defunct steel mill in the middle of nowhere. It squatted on fifteen acres. Most of its windows were shattered and its graying asphalt was cracked by weeds. Higgins had gone belly up decades ago when Chinese steel ripped their profit margin to shreds.

"Be there at…10:30 tonight. And, you d___ well better come alone. NO POLICE. Got it?"

"Yeah. I got it. How can we trust you'll bring our families and…let them go?"

"You don't trust me? That really hurts! Listen…I have no intention of hurting your families. Just…you two."

140

More silence. "10:30. BE THERE!"

* * *

Remembering the insistence that they come alone, and yet not sure leaving the FBI totally out of the loop was a good idea, Jesse deferred to Billy. "You think you should call them, you know, at least let them know about the phone call?"

"Yeah. Probably. They have ways of tracking without being seen. I'll call them."

Billy walked back to the front porch. He leaned on the railing and pulled his cell phone from his belt clip and punched in Harrelson's number. The agent answered on the third ring.

"Harrelson."

"Larry. It's me. Billy."

Billy relayed the phone call they had received from Ironman. "Ironman said, 'No police.'"

"Yeah, well, we're not police. We're FBI."

"Don't think that'll make a lot of difference to Ironman."

"I know. I know. If we decide to get involved directly, you can bet we'll be careful."

"Better do better than that, my friend. You guys screw up, who knows what Ironman might do?"

"I understand. No problem."

CHAPTER 33

Wednesday evening

8:30 p.m.

Higgins factory was sixty-six miles from Jesse's cabin. Given the terrain, it would take roughly an hour-and-a-half to get there. They were riding in Billy's truck. He figured they would arrive at about 10:00, a half-hour before their scheduled rendezvous.

For the first fifteen minutes, neither he nor Jesse spoke. Each was lost in his own thoughts of what lay ahead. "You remember how to get there?" Jesse asked, breaking the silence.

Billy didn't answer. He just nodded in the affirmative.

Wanting more clarity, Jesse said, "How? How do you know? Have you been there?"

"Yep," Billy said without taking his eyes off the road. "Me and some buddies who lived in Petros went there when we were teens. You know, just something to do. Throw a few rocks and see how many windows we could break."

"Sounds fun…not!"

The silence that had accompanied them at first, returned. An hour later, after crossing I-40, Billy glanced in the rear view mirror.

142

"I don't believe it?" he said.

"You don't believe what?"

"We're being followed. By police. Look behind you."

Jesse twisted around and fired a glance out the rear window. About a half mile behind them were four police cars, their blue lights pulsing through the night sky.

"How'd they know?" Jesse asked as he turned back around and looked at Billy.

"I don't have a clue, unless they picked up some chatter on their scanners."

*   *   *

"We got a problem, boss."

It was Snake. He and three others were sitting on their Harleys at a BP off 62 when they spotted Billy's truck and the four police cars.

"What is it," Ironman said. He and the others were already at Higgins.

"Police."

"You're kidding me, right?"

Without waiting for Snake's response, Ironman said, "D___."

*   *   *

Billy's cell phone rang. "Not too smart, guys. Guess you didn't want your families back. Did I or did I not say…NO POLICE!"

Billy hit the brakes. His truck slid to a stop leaving black marks on the shoulder. He slammed the gear shift into park. "We didn't tell the police. I have no idea how they knew."

"Well, maybe you do, maybe you don't. Doesn't make any difference. You can kiss your families goodbye." Ironman hung up.

Billy smashed his fist on the steering wheel.

"WHAT?"

Billy shared what Ironman had said.

Reminiscent of his pre-Christian days, Jesse exploded. He threw open the door, charged down the middle of the road and began waving wildly at the oncoming squad cars. Seconds later, all four screeched to a stop. The first slid sideways a mere fifteen feet in front of him.

Jesse ran up to the driver's side of the first patrol car and banged on the window. "WHAT DO YOU THINK YOU'RE DOING?"

"Calm down," the officer said as he jumped out of the squad car. His right hand was on his revolver as he stood within inches of Jesse's face. Fortunately for Jesse, they personally knew each other.

More car doors opened and slammed shut as officers from the other three cars began running toward the first patrol car and Jesse.

Billy ran up, his arms held high in a surrender position. "Sorry, guys. We're not trying to cause a problem here, but seriously…you really screwed up. Big time. We were specifically told…no police."

His hands still raised in the air, Billy said, "I just got a call from Ironman. His guys saw you coming. The exchange has been called off…because of you! If something happens to our families, I swear I'll have your badges!"

Seconds after saying that, Billy wished he hadn't. Granted, it was what he felt, but expressing what a Christian feels, especially when it's couched in anger, is counterproductive to the one thing Christians are called to do. Witness. When it comes to the importance of believing in Christ, were they ever afforded the opportunity of sharing their faith with these officers, you can bet none of them would be too receptive.

But, what was done was done. So Billy did the only thing left to do. Apologize. "Sorry, guys. Really. I didn't mean that. I know you came to help."

Five minutes later, the police turned around and headed back toward Knoxville. While standing on the shoulder, Billy pulled his cell phone from his belt clip and called Harrelson.

The agent answered on the second ring.

"Did you tell them?"

"Did I tell who…what?"

"Did you tell the Knoxville police about the exchange."

"Of course not. What are you talking about?"

145

Billy explained what had happened.

"D____. I'm sorry, man."

After a few moments of silence, Harrelson said, "Just…keep on doing what you're doing. Ironman's not going to hurt your families. He wants you guys. He'll call back. You'll see."

"I pray you're right, buddy. I pray you're right."

CHAPTER 34

Early Thursday morning.

2:45 a.m.

Ironman's cabin.

Rain angrily pelted the windows. Gusts of wind caused them to rattle and whistle. But, that wasn't what had awakened Abigail. It was the bikers. A few of them had been sitting on the back porch, talking softly. Even when cocking her ear in their direction, she couldn't quite make out what they were saying. But, in a moment of silence, she had overheard one of them say something about *offing* the Cartwrights.

Later that morning, Abigail asked her mother what that meant. Melissa explained the meaning, but couldn't bring herself to believe that Ironman would actually do that.

*   *   *

Early Friday morning.

3:00 a.m.

With the rain still pelting and rattling the windows, Abigail again lay awake. She couldn't shake the thought that—if Ironman would really off the Cartwrights, then—why not them? Why not her, her mother, Aunt Woya, Chloe and Nathan?

She had to do something, but—what? Maybe she could slip out and run for help.

Abigail sat up and glanced about the room. Her mother, Melissa, lay a couple feet to her right, curled up in a fetal position to stay warm. Nearby was aunt Woya, Chloe and Nathan. Across the room, lying on blankets and throw pillows were the Cartwrights.

About ten feet away, near the front door, was the mean one. She heard them call him Sanchez. And he *was* mean. But not as mean as the one they called boss, or Ironman. He was the meanest of all. They all seemed a little frightened of him.

Feeling that somehow, someway, she had to get help, Abigail rose. For several seconds, she just stood still, letting her eyes pan the room. Confident no one was watching, she cautiously took a couple steps toward the front door. When she was inches away from Sanchez, his body jerked and he moaned, like maybe, he was dreaming.

Abigail froze.

She held her breath.

Afraid that even the slightest movement might awaken Sanchez, she gradually let her eyes fall on him. She stood motionless for what seemed to be two minutes. Maybe more. Only when he began to breathe deeply did she look away and take a step toward the threshold. She grasped the handle of the screen door and slowly began to push it open. Swollen by moisture, it stuck at the top, then opened with a loud slapping sound.

Abigail fired a wide-eyed glance in Sanchez's direction. His eyes popped open. Still half asleep, he was momentarily confused. Then, gradually realizing what was happening, he flashed an angry stare in Abigail's direction and said, "Where do you think you're going?"

Abigail darted for the freedom of the porch, but was jerked to a halt when Sanchez grabbed her ankle. With a burst of strength born of fear, she kicked her way free, bolted through the door onto the porch, and down the steps.

"HEY..." Sanchez shouted, awakening the others. He threw off a blanket, banged through the screen door and onto the porch. Abigail was about fifty feet away when, suddenly, she slipped on the rain-slickened grass. She fell face first and slid.

As Sanchez bounded off the porch, she struggled to her feet and began to sprint toward the woods. No sooner had she entered, she began to wheeze. In her haste to get help, she had given no thought to her asthma.

Several seconds later, Sanchez entered the edge of the woods and stopped. He looked in all directions, but the darkness made it impossible to see where Abigail had gone. But soon, the rain stopped, and the moon peeked through black clouds.

Still, there was no sign of Abigail. He cocked his head to one side and listened intently for some sign of where she might be.

Then, he heard something. Like—gasping. As he neared the sound, it stopped. And then he saw her. She was lying prone on a patch of wet leaves, her face toward him. Wet strands of blond hair covered much of her face.

Sanchez towered over her. "Get up, girl!"

But—Abigail didn't get up.

Sanchez leaned forward, his hands on his knees. He nudged her shoulder. "You okay?"

When she failed to respond, Sanchez knelt beside her. He brushed the damp strands of hair from her cheek and flinched when he saw her lifeless eyes. They were wide open. Through a sliver of moonlight, he saw that the girl's face was white and her lips a purplish shade of blue.

Suddenly, he was bombarded by two powerful emotions. One was what Ironman would say. This was, after all, Jesse Striker's daughter. How would this affect the exchange once Striker discovered his only child was dead?

An equally powerful emotion was sadness. Sanchez was also a father. He had a little girl. Lucia. Although he hadn't seen her for two years, he guessed she was about the same age. She lived in Mexico City with his estranged wife.

Sanchez gently rolled Abigail on her back. He brushed away wet leaves that clung to her face. Momentarily overcome by thoughts of Lucia, he ran the sleeve of his right arm across his eyes. He took a deep breath, then gently lifted Abigail off the damp ground. With her body safely nestled in his arms, he trudged out of the woods and into the clearing.

As he neared the cabin, everyone except the Cartwrights was standing on the front porch. Woya, Chloe, Nathan, and Melissa were off to the side, near the porch swing.

When Melissa saw Sanchez slogging through the rain with Abigail in his arms, her heart stopped! She burst into tears and screamed, "ABBY!"

Melissa's scream echoed through the nearby woods as Sanchez carried Abigail up the steps to the front porch. Everyone parted as he stepped before the screen door. He yanked it open, turned sideways, and carried Abigail into the downstairs bedroom.

In shock, Melissa's knees buckled as she followed close behind. Only with Woya's help was she able to stay on her feet as she entered the bedroom behind Sanchez. He stepped up to the bed. He kicked the frame and yelled at the biker lying there. "OUT!"

Whoever it was quickly got up and left. Sanchez then gently laid Abigail's body on the bed and turned to leave. As he reached the threshold, he stopped. He looked back at Melissa and said, "I'm sorry, ma'am."

CHAPTER 35

Melissa removed a Jacob's Ladder quilt from a nearby barn board armoire and gently laid it over Abigail. She then dragged a rustic cushioned chair alongside the bed. Nearby, Woya sat on a matching chair, her feet resting upon an ottoman. Nathan was nestled in her arms; Chloe lay nearby, fast asleep on a bed of blankets.

Woya's eyes remained locked on Melissa as she sat staring at her daughter, her mind racing back in time. Like the receding, fluttering pages of a calendar, Melissa saw Abigail as she was the day she was born, all eight pounds of her. She saw her first smile just hours after her birth. Gas, the nurse had said. Not to Melissa. Then there were the birthdays. All ten of them, right up to her last, only a month ago. Tears that had ceased moments ago, returned.

Ten more minutes slugged by, until finally, Woya broke the silence. "Are you okay?"

As soon as the words came out of her mouth, Woya wished she hadn't said them. *Are you okay?* What a stupid thing to say, Woya thought. Of course she's not okay. But, what do you say to a mother whose daughter was alive one moment and dead the next? Thankfully, Melissa hadn't heard her. Her head had lolled forward and she was breathing deeply.

Believing her to be asleep, Woya closed her eyes and whispered a Cherokee prayer her father had taught her when she was five.

When she had finished, Melissa said, "That was beautiful."

"I'm sorry. I thought you were asleep."

A moment of silence passed between them. "That was a prayer in Cherokee, right?"

Woya nodded.

"What did you say?"

"I said…

Our Father, heaven dweller,
My loving will be to Thy name.
Your Lordship let it make its appearance.
Here upon earth let happen what you think,
The same as in heaven is done.
Daily our food give to us this day.
Forgive us our debts,
The same as we forgive our debtors,
And do not temptation being lead us into,
Deliver us from evil existing.
For thine your Lordship is,
And the power is,
And the glory is forever.
E-men

"The Lord's Prayer," Melissa said.

"Yes."

"Thanks. I needed that. I really did."

∗ ∗ ∗

Early Saturday morning.

3:45 a.m.

Huddled in the far corner of the living room, Roland Cartwright was whispering something to his wife, Olivia, their seventeen-year-old daughter Paige, and his brother Seth's wife, Andria. Thankfully, her daughter, Madison, was fast asleep.

Like Abigail, he had overheard the bikers saying they were going to, in their words, *off* his and Seth's family.

"We've got to do something," he whispered. "Fast."

Before he could formulate a plan, they saw Ironman and Sanchez. Both had wended their way through several bodies and were now towering over them. Neither spoke. Ironman simply glared at Cartwright. With the back of his palm toward the Warden, he wiggled his fingers indicating he wanted the Cartwrights to follow them.

Neither the Warden nor his family moved. "Where?" Roland asked.

Ironman pointed toward the back door. When they still didn't move, Ironman leaned within inches of the warden's face and whispered, "NOW!"

One by one, each of the Cartwrights followed Ironman and Sanchez onto the back porch and through a gauntlet of four ex-cons.

"Where are you taking us?" There was a quiver in the warden's voice as he spoke.

But, Ironman didn't reply as he led them off the porch. Four bikers followed behind with Sanchez last.

Walking single file, Ironman led the Cartwrights to the open barn door. They were immediately struck by the smell of gasoline-soaked hay.

"IN!" Ironman said, pointing to the dark interior of the barn.

Realizing what was about to happen, the warden spun around and faced Ironman. "YOU CAN'T DO THIS!"

Sanchez, who was now standing beside Ironman, stepped forward and slammed his open palms on the warden's chest, knocking him across the threshold. Aware of what lay ahead, each of the Cartwrights began to scream and struggle as Ironman's gang pushed them inside the barn.

One of the kidnappers forced Paige to climb the ladder to the loft. He duct taped her to a chair and doused her with gasoline.

Another biker tied the warden to a beam and forced the others to stand beside him. While they watched, screaming, he shot the warden between the eyes. He then drenched him and the others with gas.

The biker in the loft descended to the dirt floor and with the others, stepped through the barn door. Those outside walked around the barn, splashing gas on the dried boards. Then the biker who had duct taped Paige lit a match and tossed it on the trail of gas.

There was a loud WHOOSH, and the flames raced inside, engulfing those below. They charged up the ladder, snaked toward Paige, and enveloped her. Thrashing wildly and screaming, she disappeared in the flames until, mercifully, she slumped forward.

One of the Cartrights below, her body aflame, raced through the open barn door. Her flailing arms were ablaze as she shrieked in pain, stumbled, and fell on the ground before her kidnappers. Horror-stricken, they backed away from her and the heat of the inferno. A minute later, the roar of the flames completely drowned out the screams coming from within the barn.

CHAPTER 35

4:15 a.m.

Woya was the first to notice it. Flickering firelight began to dance about the bedroom. And then she heard it. It was a distant, but growing, snapping and popping sound. And—there was something else. Another sound. More frightening. Like maybe—*screams?*

"You hear that?" Woya said to Melissa, who was now wide awake.

"Hear what?"

Woya didn't answer. She jumped out of her chair and ran to the window facing the barn. "Oh my God…!"

"What?"

"THE BARN! IT'S ON FIRE!"

Melissa quickly joined Woya at the window. And remembering what Abigail had overheard, she ran to the bedroom door and threw it open. Her eyes frantically scanned the living room. But—the Cartwrights weren't there. Only six ex-cons scattered about the room—all fast asleep.

* * *

6:00 a.m.

Long after the last scream could be heard above the hissing and crackling of the fire, the ex-cons prepared to abandoned the Georgia cabin, and leave behind the smoldering remains of the barn.

"DON'T LEAVE MY BABY HERE!" Melissa screamed as Bear and Snake dragged her, Woya, Chloe and Nathan to the awaiting van. They bound and hooded each in the back. Once inside, the eleven gang members thundered away on their Harleys while Ironman drove the van.

It took nearly four hours to make the 213 mile trip to their new secure location.

As they neared it, their ears began to pop from the ever increasing elevation. At roughly 10:00 a.m., they pulled in front of a cave deep in the woods of East Tennessee.

One after another, the ex-cons shut off their Harleys and stood before the cave entrance as Ironman got out of the van and slid open the side door. As he stood before it, he glanced first at the captives, then at Sanchez. "Ricardo?"

Sanchez, who was standing with the others, turned and looked at Ironman. "Over here," Ironman said. When Sanchez neared the van, Ironman said "Cut 'em loose. And take off their hoods."

As Jesse and Billy's family exited the van, Slow Beef, Bear, and Stick ducked through the opening of the cave.

They were oblivious to the skittering of tiny rat's feet racing for darker spots from which to hide and watch.

Judging from the light that filtered in through the opening, it was clear someone had been there before. "Hey, you guys." It was Slow Beef. His voice echoed to those standing outside. "You need to see this."

The remaining bikers bent forward and entered the cave. Soon they all saw what Slow Beef had seen. Before them, covered with years of dust, were a rough, hand-hewn log table, chair, and bed. "Look's like someone got here before we did," Snake said.

"Someone did." It was Ironman. Along with Woya, Chloe, Nathan, and Melissa, he had just ducked inside the cave. He stood, and with his hands on his hips and his back toward the opening, he said, "Mason Evans."

"Who?" asked Bear.

Ironman had hated school. One reason was that he had spent most of it in a Georgia reform school. Fortunately, he got his GED. Even so, he hated every subject save one. History. Over the years, he devoured ancient, European, and American history. He especially loved local history. Living in the Georgia / Tennessee area, he was familiar with much of it, including the tales of the hermit, Mason Evans.

Rejected in love, as a young man in his twenties, Evans had fled to the mountains of the Cherokee National Forest in northeastern Tennessee. He lived in this very cave until he died of exposure at the age of sixty-eight.

When he had finished sharing the story of Mason Evans, one of the ex-cons sarcastically said, "Well, what a beautiful story. So…what's that got to do with us? We ain't staying here are we?"

The one asking was Will Johnson. At five-foot-five, Johnson was one of three ex-cons who didn't have, or want, a biker name. With the defiance gained by years of being bullied, he had been quick to remind others that— as the cliché goes— "It's not the size of the dog in the fight, it's the size of the fight in the dog."

"Yeah," asked Snake. "We aren't…are we?"

"Nope," Ironman said as he turned to leave the cave. "This way." As they followed him and stood outside the cave entrance, they looked in the direction Ironman was pointing. "Over there."

CHAPTER 36

There was a moment of silence as they all stared into the dense undergrowth. The rays of early morning sunlight were few and far between. That, plus the vegetation, made it impossible to see much of anything.

"Over where?" asked Bear. "I don't see nothing."

About a hundred yards away, hidden in vegetation and surrounded by kudzu, were the remains of an old log cabin. Kudzu, which might be dubbed the flora version of the anaconda—surrounds, strangles and suffocates its victims. That included the remains of several Virginia pines and a smattering of tulip trees that surrounded the cabin. Stripped of all vegetation, they stood at dead attention.

"That's...our home?" Bear asked.

"Yep," Ironman said. "For now."

Following his lead, they all walked to the cabin and stepped onto the front porch. Ironman pulled on the door, but it didn't budge. Age and moisture had warped it out of joint, causing it to bite into the floor boards. Lifting the wooden handle, he was able to scrape it open.

Stepping inside, they all stood and inspected their new home. With the exception of a handmade dust covered table, four chairs and one bed, the two-room cabin was bare. A blackened stone fireplace was centered on the north wall. Beside it, on the left, ten steps rose, turned right and climbed to a loft.

Pointing to it, Ironman said to Melissa, Woya and her children, "Ladies and kiddies, that's where you're going to stay. You might as well check it out."

As they climbed the steps to the loft, Big Guy said, "How old is this cabin?"

"H___ if I know," Ironman said. "If I had to guess, I'd say it's at least hundred years old.

"I don't see how," Snake said, his eyes locked on a single light bulb that hung in the center of the room. "Don't think they had electrified cabins a hundred years ago."

"Maybe somebody stayed here since then and made some improvements," Bear said.

"Well, if there's a bulb, there's a generator," said Ironman. "There's a tool shed outside." To Snake he said, "Go see if you can find it."

Snake did. When he returned, he said, "Yep. There's a generator. And a large can of gas."

"Well, go back and see if the d___ thing works."

"Get someone else to do it."

Ironman just pointed toward the door. Needing no further encouragement, Snake returned to the tool shed. Within five minutes, the bare bulb in the main room, slowly began to glow.

Before returning, Snake noticed a storm door lying flat on the ground. It was perpendicular to the cabin. He pulled it open, revealing several chipped concrete steps. They led down to another door. Snake cautiously walked down the steps and pulled it open. Immediately, he was assaulted by the musty smell of mildew. And—it was dark. Real dark.

Snake pulled a lighter from his leather vest and struck it. Immediately, the flickering light revealed a dirt floor, a soiled couch, and a rusted single bed frame.

"Hey," Snake said, as he returned. "Did you know there's a root cellar?"

"I do now," Ironman said.

"You guys?" It was Bull. He was squinting through the dust and cobwebs of a side window. "What do you know. All the comforts of home. We got us an outhouse."

"Sanchez," Ironman said. "Take the van and a couple guys and get us some food. While you're at it, pick up a couple cases of beer." He handed Sanchez a list, some cash, and gave him directions to nearby Etowah.

In the minutes that followed, each ex-con selected a little corner to call his own while Ironman stepped onto the front porch, sat on the top step and lit a joint. A few minutes later, Snake joined him. "What do we do next?"

Ironman took another drag on his joint then said, "In a few days, we'll head for Chilhowee State Prison, or— what remains of it."

CHAPTER 37

Saturday morning.

10:45 a.m.

Jesse's cabin.

Jesse was in the kitchen, putting his and Billy's breakfast plates in the dish washer. Billy was on the front porch, drinking his second cup of coffee when his cell phone rang.

Upon hearing it, Jesse quickly joined Billy on the porch and mouthed the words, "Who is it?"

Billy just shrugged. "Hello?"

"Billy?"

"Yeah. Who's this?"

"It's me. Larry."

"Oh. Hi Larry. You got something?"

"I'm not sure. Maybe. There was a big fire in North Georgia last night, about forty or so miles from Macon. Our guys discovered that it was in the area where there's a cabin owned by the former senator of Vermont…"

"Purdue? Robert Purdue?"

"Yeah. How'd you know?"

"Jesse confronted him twelve years ago. He's the reason Purdue resigned."

"So, you know he's the father of Beau Haggart, alias…
Ironman."

"I do."

"Well, it's just a guess, or call it intuition, but maybe…
just maybe…that's where he's got your families."

"Are you gonna' check it out…right?"

"Of course."

"We want to go with you."

"Impossible."

"Larry, I've known you for a long time. You know
how to pull strings. Make it possible."

There was a moment of silence.

"Okay…okay. You and Jesse meet us at the FBI
hanger at McGhee Tyson at 11:30. We'll chopper over the
cabin and see what we can see."

＊　＊　＊

The Knoxville FBI office had access to two helicop-
ters, a refurbished Hughes MD 500 chopper and the
larger Sikorsky Black Hawk helicopter. They chose the
smaller MD 500 for this mission. Given its cruising speed
of 145 miles-per-hour and the distance from Knoxville to
the cabin of 154 miles, it would take a little over an hour
to reach their destination.

The MD 500, which had been configured to accommodate seven passengers, was filled to capacity. Besides
the pilot, there was Harrelson, Billy, Jesse and the three
agents. Following GPS coordinates, an hour and ten

minutes later, they hovered over the site of the fire. Wiggling trails of smoke were still rising from the blackened and ash gray remains of the barn.

"See that?" Harrelson said over the mike. He was pointing to the nearby structure. "That's got to be the senator's cabin."

Below them were two fire engines, two local and one county police car, and a couple Georgia State Police vehicles. Ten or more officers and firefighters were milling about the site.

"Set her down, Mike," Harrelson said to the pilot.

A few minutes later, while Mike shut down the engine, his six passengers ducked beneath the rotating wings of the chopper and hurried toward what was left of the barn.

Harrelson walked up to the state trooper who seemed in charge. He pulled his billfold from his hip pocket and flashed his FBI badge. "What have you found so far?"

The officer looked at the badge, Harrelson, and then Billy and Jesse who were standing on either side of him.

"Captain Montgomery," he said, holding out his hand to Harrelson. "It's bad." Shaking his head he added, "We've found five bodies."

"Men, women, or children?"

"Can't tell for sure. Whoever torched this barn used a lot of gasoline. The bodies are charred beyond recognition. But…judging from the size, I'd say there was one child and four adults."

While the three other FBI agents joined those sifting through the remains of the barn, Harrelson pulled Billy and Jesse to one side. "If this is where Ironman was holding your families and the Cartwrights, that would make ten people. But there are only five bodies in the barn. I've got to believe they're the five Cartwrights, the warden, his wife and daughter, and his brother's wife and their daughter.

"Besides, it doesn't make sense that Ironman would harm your families. I mean, he wants you guys, and he d___ well knows he's not going to be able to make an exchange without them. You agree?"

Feeling a measure of relief sweep over him, Jesse momentarily closed his eyes, took a deep breath, and said, "I do."

"Billy?"

"Yeah. Me too. Thank God!"

Just then, Captain Montgomery yelled at one of his officers, "Brady, check the cabin."

Harrelson, Billy, and Jesse were standing about fifty feet away. They looked on as the officer entered the cabin. A minute later, they saw him rushing out the front door. "You better come here, sir. We've got a body. A young girl!"

Jesse's head snapped in Billy's direction and then he began sprinting toward the cabin. Billy followed close behind.

Jesse bounded up the steps and dashed through the open door. He stopped momentarily, and upon hearing the officers voices coming from a bedroom, he burst between them and—froze.

He was instantly in shock as he saw what no father should see. His daughter, Abigail, lay on the bed. Her face was pale and her lips were blue. Abby—was dead.

"NOOOOOOOOO!" Jesse screamed. He fell to his knees beside Abigail. Through glazed eyes, he felt for a pulse, but there was none. "ABBY…ABBY," he yelled as he threw his arms around her cool body and gently shook here. "WAKE UP BABY…WAKE UP!"

Even as he said those words, he knew better. Abby was not going to wake up, at least, not on this side of heaven.

Still on his knees, Jesse buried his head in his hands, and sobbed.

A couple minutes later, Billy stepped beside him and helped him to his feet. Jesse wiped his eyes and said to no one, "I'm not going to leave her."

"Neither would I. Let's take her home." Billy said.

Billy carefully wrapped Abigail's body in the quilt and gently placed her in Jesse's open arms. Together, they, Harrelson, the three agents, and the pilot walked back to the helicopter.

* * *

It was 4:15 when the chopper landed at McGhee Tyson. Jesse gently laid Abigail's body on the back seat of Billy's truck. He sat beside her as Billy drove them to Sevierville and the Anderson Funeral Home.

Jesse entered with Abigail in his arms. Billy was right behind him. When Jesse's friend and owner, Jim Anderson, saw Jesse carrying Abigail's lifeless body, he said, "Oh my God…what's happened?"

Jesse started to tell him but, choked up. Billy relayed the events of the past week.

"I'm so sorry, Jesse. How can I help?"

Jesse took a deep breath. He gently laid Abigail's body on a nearby couch, and turning to Anderson, he said, "Please, just…hold Abby's body until we get Melissa back so we can both bury her. Can you do that?"

"If course…of course. That's no problem, Jesse."

Jesse thanked him, turned, took one last look at his daughter, and then left with Billy.

CHAPTER 38

Sunday afternoon.

4:20 p.m.

Jesse's cabin.

The loss Jesse felt over Abigail's death, coupled with the kidnapping of Melissa, was the lowest point of his life. It was matched only by the tragic murder of his first wife, Jenny. His greatest fear now was that maybe, even Melissa—like Jenny and Abigail, might also be—

Jesse didn't want to finish that thought. How does one deal with that? The three persons you have loved more than life itself—suddenly gone?

Jesse was sitting on one of the twin rockers on his back porch. Though nearly imperceptible, his right leg was bouncing up and down.

Billy sat nearby on the swing. Ever since they had arrived at Jesse's, neither had spoken more than three words. Each was lost in his own thoughts when Jesse's cell phone dinged. The sound hit Jesse like a slap and he jerked.

Someone had sent him a video.

Billy got up from the swing and pulled the matching rocker closer as Jesse hit the play button.

It was a video of the barn. It was ablaze. A cell phone camera panned to the right, and—there was Woya, Chloe, Nathan, and Melissa. Everyone—except Abigail. Now, he knew why.

Although nearly drowned out by the roar of the fire, they could also hear someone speaking. They couldn't make out the words, but it sounded like it might be Ironman's voice.

Feeling a measure of relief and hoping to comfort Jesse, Billy said, "That's proof, Jesse. Melissa is alive. So is Woya and my kids."

"Yeah. Well…at least they were when the video was taken."

"Jesse, think about it. Who took this video, and why? It had to be one of Ironman's gang. Who else? And why would they do it if not to reassure us that Melissa, Woya, Chloe and Nathan are still alive.

"Jesse, I don't know what happened to Abigail, but I don't believe for a minute they purposely hurt her. For that matter, I don't think they would hurt Melissa or my family. They'd be screwed. They'd have no chance of swapping them for us, and they've got to know that."

After a pause, Jesse said, "Maybe you're right. I pray so."

"I think we should let Harrelson view the video. You heard the voice in the background. Maybe if we know for sure who it is, and what he was saying, we'd be a step closer to finding where they are."

His hope somewhat buoyed, Jesse said, "I agree."

"I'll give him a call." Billy took out his cell phone and placed the call.

Three rings later—

"Harrelson."

"Larry, it's me." Billy shared what was on the video.

"Can you guys bring it to my office? We need to run it through our voice recognition software and see if the voice you heard, or thought you heard, is Ironman."

"Sure. When?" Billy said.

"Can you be here in the morning, say…at 9:00?"

"We'll be there."

*　*　*

Monday morning.

FBI headquarters.

9:00 a.m.

"Show me what you got," Harrelson said as Billy and Jesse entered the agent's glass-enclosed cubical. Jesse handed his cell phone to Harrelson, who said, "Follow me."

Harrelson led Jesse and Billy down a hall to a windowless room full of electronic equipment. An officer sitting behind several monitors spun around in his chair. "This is Jim Watson," Harrelson said. "He's an IT specialist on loan from the Tennessee Bureau of Investigation. He's helping Peterson on some of our cases.

They greeted one another and Harrelson handed Watson Jesse's phone. Watson spun back around and quickly copied the video file into the voice recognition program while Harrelson, Billy, and Jesse stood behind him, looking over his shoulder.

"How's this thing work?" Jesse asked.

With his face locked on the screen and his fingers flicking switches and turning knobs, Watson said, "Well, speaker recognition systems have two phases: enrollment and verification. During enrollment, the speaker's voice is recorded and typically a number of features are extracted to form a voice print, template, or model."

Jesse looked at Billy with a "What's he sayin'?" look, then back at Watson.

"In the verification phase, a speech sample or utterance is compared against a previously created voice print. For identification systems, the utterance is compared against multiple voice prints in order to determine the best match while verification systems compare an utterance against a single voice print. Because of the process involved, verification is faster than identification. That's to our advantage since we are simply comparing the subject's voice from a prison recording to the voice on your video to see if they're the same."

Jesse looked at Billy for a second time, squinted, and said, "I don't get it." To Watson he said, "Maybe…I don't need to know how it works."

Watson turned in his chair and facing Billy and Jesse said, "Larry's filled me in on your case. So, let's just say, I'm going to compare the two files and see if the voice at the site of the burning barn is Beau Haggart. Watson turned back to the monitor and began the recognition process. Three minutes later, he spun around in his chair and said, "It's a match."

Harrelson, Billy, and Jesse looked at one another. "There's your proof," Harrelson said. "Ironman *was* at the cabin, and it's a good bet, he held the Cartwrights and your families there. And you can bet he still has your families, somewhere. The question is…where."

"Jim," Billy said. "If you don't mind, play the video again."

As he did, they could again clearly hear the crackling, popping, and hissing of the roaring fire. They again heard what they now knew was Ironman's voice. But this time, they heard something else. Another voice. It sounded as if someone was asking Ironman a question.

"Did you hear that?" Billy asked.

Watson backed up the tape and turned some knobs to further clarify the sound. "You're right. There *is* another voice. I can't make out the exact words, but whoever it is seems to be asking Ironman a question."

"Play it again," Jesse said."

Watson did. Only three words were recognizable. Going to…and…Star…"

"What could that possibly mean?" Jesse asked.

174

"My guess is, Ironman and his gang left and took your families somewhere," Harrelson said. "Maybe somewhere has something to do with...*Star.*"

After a moment of silence, Harrelson said, "I've got an idea." He stepped out of the room and a minute later returned with a guy who couldn't have been more than thirty, but looked much older, thanks to his nearly bald pate. Harrelson introduced him to Billy and Jesse.

"This is Todd Ferguson. He's with the Chattanooga office. Like Watson, he's on loan. In any case, nearly all of us here are transplants from up north. But Todd's a native, born and bred in Hamilton County. It struck me that the word *star* might mean something to him."

Watson played the video for Ferguson, pointing out the word *star.*

Harrelson asked Todd, "Does that mean anything to you?"

"As a matter of fact, it does. Star...S-T-A-R-R...two 'R's, as in—Starr Mountain."

CHAPTER 39

Located seventy-two miles southwest of Knoxville, Starr Mountain is a high flat plateau halfway between Tellico Plains and Etowah, Tennessee. In the latter days of the Cherokee Nation, it was the home of Caleb Starr. Like many men living in East Tennessee and Western North Carolina, Caleb married a Cherokee girl. Her name was Nancy Harlan. She was the granddaughter of Nancy Ward and thus quite prominent among the Cherokees.

Caleb and Nancy had twelve children. One was James Starr. In 1835, he and others signed the infamous "Treaty of New Echota" that led to the expulsion of the Cherokees from their homeland. Over sixteen-thousand Cherokee men, women, and children were forced to march over one thousand miles to a reservation in Oklahoma. It would be called, "The Trail of Tears." More than five-thousand didn't make it; they died of exposure, starvation, and disease.

Caleb, who was eighty at the time, and his aging wife Nancy, survived. Upon their deaths, they were buried at Oak Grove Cemetery in Lincoln County, Oklahoma.

Their Starr Mountain home—surrounded as it was by valleys, ravines, bogs, waterfalls, thick forests and impenetrable undergrowth—not to mention the

century old abandoned Chilhowee State Prison cam-
ouflaged nearby—was the perfect place to exchange the
Whitecloud and Striker families for Billy and Jesse.

* * *

Friday morning.

5:00 a.m.

Billy and Jesse began to fear the worst as five days
dragged by without any word from Ironman. When
finally he did call, both were fast asleep. Jesse, who slept in
the downstairs bedroom, was the first to hear the phone.
He jerked awake and sat up. Momentarily locked in that
transitional place between the subconscious and conscious mind, he wasn't fully aware of what had awakened
him until—his cell phone rang a third time.

Jesse fumbled for his phone, snatched it from the end
table and said, "Yeah?"

"Sounds like I'm talking to Jesse Striker."

"You are." Jesse's voice sounded like he had a mouth-
ful of gravel. "Who are you?"

"You don't recognize my voice by now? I'm
disappointed."

"IRONMAN?"

"In person."

"What have you done to our families?"

"They're doing just fine. Enjoying their time away
from you guys. You know how it is? Now listen…if you
want your families back, I want you and the chief to meet

177

us at the abandoned Chilhowee Prison, tomorrow evening at 10:00. You know where it is?"

"I do. Where will we find you?"

"Don't worry. You just enter the prison's main entrance. We'll find you."

*   *   *

Chilhowee State Prison lay desolate on a thirty acre wooded area five miles outside Tellico Plains. Not far from Starr Mountain, it was decommissioned in 1932 during the early years of the depression. A winding, twisting, rising and falling, two mile road was then, and now, the only way in. It's still accessible, though just barely. Wild vegetation covers most of what remains of the gravel road. During heavy rains, lower segments of what's left of the road become muddy, passable only by four-wheel drive vehicles.

Today, seventy to one hundred foot loblolly pines, a few tulip trees and a smattering of white pines surround and block one's view of the prison. Only as one nears the now fallen, rusted chain link entrance gate, can one see the skeleton of the prison.

Following a 6:30 supper at Jesse's cabin, he and Billy had retired on the back porch, each with a cup of coffee. "I think we should fill in Harrelson about the exchange," Billy said.

"I agree."

Billy, who was sitting on the swing, set his coffee on the log end table and hit Harrelson's speed dial number. It rang four times and was followed by the agent's 'I'm-not-here' message. *This is Agent Harrelson. I'm not able to come to the phone right now. Leave a message and I'll get back to you. If it's an emergency, call 911.*

"Larry. Call me. It's important."

A half hour later, at roughly 7:00, Harrelson called.

"What's up?"

"We've heard from Ironman. He's set up an exchange for tomorrow evening."

"Where?"

"The old Chilhowee Prison."

"The one that's been closed for...who knows how long?"

"One and the same."

"Okay. May I make a suggestion?"

"Would it make any difference if I said no?"

"No."

"Okay. What's your suggestion?"

"Don't go alone."

"We've been down that road before."

"Hear me out. If there's trouble, and there's always trouble when Haggart's involved, you're going to need backup. I suggest we lead the way and park outside the entrance gate while you follow behind. We'll wait there while you guys go on in. We'll equip each of you with pager-sized police-cams with night vision and audio capability. That way we can monitor what's going on. If you get in any trouble, we'll be close by. Sound okay?"

"Yeah. That'll work."

"Good. Meet us at the Knoxville office tomorrow evening at 7:45."

"Will do. Thanks, Larry."

"No thanks needed. We just want to get your families back safe and sound."

"You and us both!"

CHAPTER 40

Saturday.

8:00 p.m.

Director Harrelson and agents Peterson, McGill, and Takara rode in the FBI's Land Rover. Billy and Jesse followed behind in Billy's truck. With the audio capacity of their police cam, both were able to stay in contact with the agents by a touch of the transmit button on their earpieces.

While on route, Harrelson pressed his. "Where are you guys?"

Unfamiliar with the road, Billy and Jesse had lagged far behind. Making it even more difficult, they were surrounded by the dense vegetation and tall loblolly and Virginia pines. Even with the full moon, visibility was a challenge.

From the passenger seat, Jesse responded. "We're behind you, just bouncing along. Every now and then, we see your taillights."

"Okay, listen…we're about a half-mile from the entrance gate. As I recall, there's a pull off on the right. We're going to back into it and wait for Ironman. You guys go on ahead. When they come by, we'll try to see if he's brought your families. Either way, we'll give you a heads up."

"Roger," Jesse said.

Not knowing whether Harrelson or the other agents were Christian, Jesse nonetheless said, "While you're waiting, you might spend some time praying that this all works out."

Harrelson didn't respond, which to Jesse, suggested that praying might not be a high priority for him. To fill the silence that followed, Jesse added, "Either way, you can bet we'll be praying like crazy."

About seven minutes later, Harrelson blinked his headlights as Billy and Jesse approached the pull off. Billy did the same. With his eyes locked on the rutted road ahead, he continued to aim his Ram 1500 down the remaining quarter-mile of the Chilhowee Prison Road.

Soon, they could see segments of the ten-foot, chain link fence on both sides of where the gate should be. It was clearly missing. They quickly discovered that it lay hidden on the ground with sprigs of grass poking through.

Slowly, Billy eased the truck over the gate. Rusted chain links snapped and crunched beneath the tires as the truck shimmied over its remains. Once on the other side, Billy hit the brakes and stopped.

There, a football field away, surrounded by knee-high grass, loomed the Chilhowee State Prison. Bathed in moonlight and illuminated by the truck's headlights, they could make out its flaking, dull red brick, its color eaten away by time and the elements. Two rows of rust covered, metal windows ran the length of the 500 foot, two-story structure.

As they sat mesmerized by the gloomy skeleton of the prison, Jesse said, "Kind of reminds me of *The Walking Dead*. You know? The TV series?"

Billy cast a quick glance in Jesse's direction. "Yeah. I know. Thanks, Jesse," he said ironically. "That's…a real comforting thought."

Actually, though in no way comforting, it felt good to be distracted from what lay ahead, if even for a moment.

"Let's do it," Billy said. He shifted the truck into gear and they began to edge closer to the main entrance. As they neared it, light from the full moon reflected off the cracked and broken shards of glass that remained in the windows.

Ten feet from the entrance, Billy stopped the truck. He turned off the engine and shut off the headlights. Jesse grabbed a flashlight and both he and Billy got out.

The first thing they noticed was the silence. It was the kind one experiences only in the country, far from highways and industries. Piercing it was the chirping of crickets. Thousands of crickets. They were accompanied by the faint croaking of frogs from a nearby bog.

Billy and Jesse surveyed their surroundings. They looked in all directions and listened intently for any sounds that might suggest someone was already there.

Hearing none, they warily stepped up to the thick metal door. It had been pried open, no doubt by some curious youth, possibly looking for a Halloween thrill.

"Here goes nothing," Jesse said as he sidled through the narrow opening and stepped over the threshold. Billy was close behind.

Immediately, cave-like, claustrophobic darkness enveloped them. It was what one might feel were they to wake up alive in a casket buried six feet under the ground.

But slowly, thankfully, their eyes gradually adjusted to the darkness. Jesse flicked on the flashlight while Billy pressed the transmit button on his earpiece and said, "We're in."

Harrelson responded. "Roger."

CHAPTER 41

"You guys have at least an hour to kill," Harrelson said. "Maybe more, maybe less. I think it would be wise to become familiar with your surroundings."

Jesse toggled the transmit switch. "Agreed."

The room they were standing in was some kind of foyer, maybe twenty-five by thirty-feet and twelve feet high. The sides were cinder blocks that appeared to have once been painted battleship gray. On both sides, there were lighter gray rectangular areas where, presumably, pictures of the governor and the warden may have at one time greeted visitors.

Jesse looked upward and pointed the flashlight toward the ceiling, only—there was no ceiling. Only rusted grids. Whatever tiles had been there had long ago been removed.

Topping the cinder blocks on both sides and running the full length were three rows of glass window blocks. And in front, in the center of the cinder block wall was an open, iron bar gate.

"Lovely," Jesse said to himself. To Billy he added, "You want to lead the way, Sherlock."

"You've got the flashlight."

"So I do." Jesse stepped through the bars and into the two story cell block. Billy walked beside him. The damp interior was permeated with the smell of mildew. And there was the slight stench of dead animals that had wandered inside, drew their last breath, and decayed.

Jesse and Billy slid their dual lens, night vision goggles down, instantly transforming the cell block to an eerie shade of green. Were one to let his imagination run wild, he might catch a glimpse of the ghosts of caged humans, some standing in front of their second floor cells, leaning on the iron railing, others roaming about.

Jesse shivered, as if to unconsciously shake away that ridiculous thought. And with his flashlight poking about and leading the way, he and Billy began to walk down the center of the cell block. On their right and left were two tiers of cells reaching to the ceiling some fifty feet above.

Jesse pressed his ear mike. "You guys see what we're seeing?"

"We do. But it would help if you'd also describe it."

"Okay. We're in the center of the cell block. We're walking toward the far end. On the right of the far wall is a stairwell leading downward. You see it?"

"We do."

There was a moment of silence as Jesse and Billy walked toward it. Seconds later, standing before the stairwell, Jesse said, "Looks like it leads down to an underground level."

Jesse and Billy descended the steps. When they reached the bottom, Jesse said, "We're in a long, narrow hall, maybe fifty feet in length. On both sides are prison cells. On the outside door of each is a small barred window. And above us, running down the length of the hall are…let me count them…eight wire-encased shields that once held light bulbs."

To Billy, Jesse said, "You think this might have been… death row?"

"Could be."

"I can't imagine being down here," Jesse said. "I think it would drive me crazy. Check that, I *know* it would drive me crazy." A second later, he said, "What's that?" Jesse was pointing the beam of his flashlight on a circular opening on the floor. It was centered in front of the far wall. It resembled a manhole leading to a sewer, only there was no cover.

"What are you seeing?" asked Harrelson.

Jesse stepped near the opening. He pointed the beam of his flashlight down it and said, "It's a hole in the floor, about…I'd say, three foot in diameter. There's a vertical ladder that descends downward about, maybe…fifteen feet."

To Billy, Jesse said, "I don't even want to think what's down there. Why don't you go first?" Billy just shook his head. When Jesse panned the beam of light on his face, it revealed the hint of a smile.

"Okay...okay." Jesse said as he climbed into the hole and down the steps. "You comin'?"

"What do you think?"

Upon reaching the bottom, Jesse pressed his mike and said, "You guys see what we see." Without waiting for a response, he continued, "We're another fifteen or so feet below the floor above. This room is like it, only smaller. There are eight cells, four on each side. There are no windows. I suspect it's too far beneath the ground. And there are no bars. Just solid metal doors with a rectangular opening large enough to slip food through."

Jesse pointed the flashlight inside one of the open cells. Beside a concrete bed with the remains of a tattered, soiled mattress, were a sink and a hole."

With his flashlight focused on the hole, he said to Billy, "You don't think...?"

"...That, that's a toilet? I do believe it is."

"You guys see this?" Jesse said to Harrelson and the guys outside. "What do you think this room is?"

"My best guess?" answered Harrelson? "Solitary confinement."

Just then, a voice from above boomed down the hole. "WELCOME GUYS. SO GOOD TO SEE YOU!"

There was no mistaking that voice. It was—Ironman.

CHAPTER 42

Harrelson sprang to attention when he heard the voice of Ironman. "D___! We've got a problem guys. Big time. Obviously, Ironman is not coming. He's here. In the prison." Harrelson threw open the door and slid out. "LET'S GO!"

The three agents who had accompanied him: Peterson, McGill, and Takara quickly exited the Land Rover and began running toward the prison.

* * *

"WHERE ARE OUR FAMILIES?"Billy demanded. "YOU SAID THIS WAS AN EXCHANGE. US FOR OUR FAMILIES!"

"I did say that, didn't I?" Ironman stood erect. Smiling, he turned around and faced the three who had accompanied him: Snake, Bear, and Big Guy, who, at six-five and 290 pounds, was actually bigger than Bear.

Peering back down the hole, Ironman said, "Well, let's just say…I lied. So…why don't you boys just climb out of your hole and we'll settle things."

Knowing that Harrelson and the other agents had heard everything, Jesse stalled for time. "If you think we came unarmed, you're crazy. Why don't *you* come down

189

the hole, and we'll pick you off one-by-one. You know, like shooting fish in a barrel."

"Well, you do that, how will you ever know where your families are?"

"How do we even know our families are still alive?" Billy asked.

"You don't. But…they are."

"Prove it. Drop them off at the Knoxville Police Department. And when we receive a call from Chief Bradley assuring us they are safe, we'll come up."

"Well, that sounds fair, and…I am a fair man. Let's deal with the proof first."

"You boys got your cell phones, I presume."

When Jesse acknowledged they did, Ironman called Sanchez who—along with the other ex-cons—was at the Starr Mountain cabin, watching Billy and Jesse's families.

"Sanchez. This is Ironman. Get the families. I want you to do a FaceTime video so our boys can see their families are alive and well."

Sanchez did as he was told, and soon, Woya got on the phone.

As Billy and Jesse stared at Jesse's phone, both were momentarily speechless. When Billy did speak, his voice cracked. "Honey, it's so good to see you and… hear your voice. We're going to get you back home soon. Just…just hang on a little."

"I will. How are *you* doing?"

"I'm okay. Better than okay now I know you're alive."

"Where are you?"

"I can't say right now."

"Will I see you soon?"

Billy paused. "Yeah, soon," he lied. "I love you, hon!"

"I love you too."

"I can't stay on the phone long. Put Chloe and Nathan on. Okay?"

"Okay," Woya said as she handed the cell phone to Chloe.

After talking briefly with his kids, Billy said to Nathan, "Put Melissa on, Nate."

Nathan gave the phone to Melissa while Billy handed the phone to Jesse.

"Melissa…sweetheart, I miss you so much," Jesse said. "Are you okay?"

"I will be when I see you again."

"I love you, baby!"

"Jesse…? I need to tell you something…" There was a catch in Melissa's voice.

Afraid she was about to mention Abigail's death and unaware that Jesse already knew, Sanchez snatched the phone from Melissa and turned it off.

CHAPTER 43

Harrelson and the three agents slowed as they reached the door to the prison. Not knowing whether one of Ironman's gang might be outside, they froze and scanned the area. Seeing no one, Harrelson pointed to his night vision goggles and pulled them down, signaling the others to do the same.

"Masumi," he said, "I want you to go around back."

"Roger."

Harrelson then nodded toward the partially open metal door and he, Peterson and McGill slipped inside. They passed through the foyer and stepped into the murky cell block, turned left and stopped. Harrelson pressed the transmit button on his earpiece and whispered to Jesse and Billy, "We're inside."

"Copy that," Billy whispered.

The three agents continued to warily walk down the center of the cell block. Their eyes raked the first and second floor cells on both sides, looking for any sign of movement. For all they knew, one of Ironman's thugs was standing on the second floor eyeing them through a scope of a high powered rifle.

To hopefully dismiss that possibility, the three agents continued to search the lower and upper cells through the green haze of their goggles.

Thirty seconds.

Forty.

Seeing no one, Harrelson again triggered his mike. "Masumi…where are you now?"

"I'm out back, about in the center of the building."

"What do you see?"

"There's a metal door just a little to my left."

"That's probably the exit from the cell block. What else do you see?"

"Just a minute. Let me move a little closer."

Seconds later, Masumi said, "I'm looking at some concrete steps on my right. They descend downward…I'd say…about twenty feet. There's a metal door at the bottom."

Harrelson whispered to Peterson and McGill. "That may be the door to the long hall just below the cell block. The one Billy thought might be death row."

"Okay," Harrelson said to Masumi. "Stay put and keep your eyes open."

"Roger."

From what they had seen through Billy and Jesse's night vision goggles and from overhearing them, the agents had a good idea of what was before them.

At the far end of the first floor cell block, on the right, were the steps leading down to a lower floor. And near the far end of that, a hole leading to an even lower level. Billy and Jesse had climbed down a ladder to that third level.

If the agents had understood correctly, Ironman and a few of his ex-cons were standing near that hole on the floor directly below them. Harrelson eyed Peterson and McGill. He pointed toward the steps leading down to where they believed Ironman was, and they began to slowly make their way toward it.

With each step, they were painfully aware of the gritty sound of years of layered dust and minute pieces of the crumbling concrete floor. Hopefully, it wasn't loud enough for anyone to hear.

Seconds later, they were standing before the steps leading down to the next level.

Unexpectedly, McGill stepped on something. A loose piece of concrete flooring perhaps. Whatever it was, it dislodged and clattered down the steps. Like a stone skipping on water, it bounced two, three, four, then five times and rolled to a stop on the hallway below.

* * *

Ironman's head snapped around. His eyes locked on the stairwell. "WHO'S THERE?"

Harrelson yelled back. "FBI! DROP YOUR WEAPONS!"

"GO TO H___," shouted Ironman, and pulling his 38 snub nose revolver from its holster, he fired a round in the direction of the stairwell.

The blast echoed off the cinderblock walls, struck the side of the stairwell, and ricocheted upward, striking Peterson in the head. His body fell to the concrete floor like a marionette whose strings had been suddenly cut.

CHAPTER 44

"Man down," Harrelson yelled on his mike. It was not a call for help, as was usually the case. He had said it more out of habit. It would take hours for EMT's to arrive at Chilhowee. Even if they could apparate, it would do no good. Agent Peterson was beyond help. The bullet had struck him between the eyes, instantly transporting him to wherever his faith, or lack of it, would take him.

His ears still ringing from the gunshot, Billy touched his finger to his earpiece, triggering the mike. "WHAT'S HAPPENING?"

Harrelson quickly explained that Peterson was dead. He then said, "Is Ironman still on the floor above you?"

"I don't know!" To hopefully discover his whereabouts, Billy yelled, "IRONMAN! YOU'RE IN BIG TROUBLE. YOU JUST KILLED AN FBI AGENT!"

There was no response.

To Harrelson, Billy said, "I don't think he's still here, but I don't have any idea where he or the others could have gone. Certainly not back in your direction."

"I think I know where they are, or...where they'll soon be." It was Masumi speaking from the back of the prison. "If those concrete steps I told you about lead to the floor Ironman was on, I wouldn't be surprised to see him and whoever's with him, coming up them at any moment. One other thing, since I last spoke with you, I discovered a black van. It's hidden behind an outbuilding. I suspect that might be where they'll be heading."

There was a moment of silence, then Masumi whispered into her mike. "They're coming up the steps."

Her pistol outstretched before her, Masumi shouted at Ironman as he and three ex-cons stood at the top of the steps.

"FBI! PUT YOUR HANDS UP!"

That was the last thing Masumi Takara would ever speak. Fire erupted from Ironman's revolver. It struck Masumi in the right shoulder and spun her around. A second bullet sliced through her neck and she fell to the ground.

From inside the prison, Harrelson, McGill, Billy, and Jesse heard the muffled shots.

"MASUMI?" Harrelson yelled in his mike.

Hearing nothing, he called out again, "MASUMI, ARE YOU OKAY?"

Harrelson's head snapped in McGill's direction. And then to Billy and Jesse he said, "I'm afraid Takara's down."

Harrelson turned and began racing through the cell block, on his way to the front door. With one finger pressed to his earpiece, his voice sputtered in and out. To Billy and Jesse, he said, "ONE OF YOU GUYS CHECK ON MASUMI... WE'RE... GOING... OUT FRONT...!"

197

Billy and Jesse clambered up the ladder and through the hole to the death row floor. Once there, Jesse said to Billy, "I'LL CHECK ON MASUMI!"

Billy nodded, spun around, and headed up the steps and through the cell block, on his way to the front. Jesse raced for the side door that led to the back. He burst through it and clambered up the concrete steps, two at a time. When he reached the top, his eyes were immediately drawn to the taillights of the black van as it slid out of view, headed for the front. He then saw Masumi lying on the ground.

He had no way of knowing that Adryel was also there. He was towering over her.

Jesse ran up to Masumi and knelt. He felt for a pulse and was relieved to find that she was still alive.

"Jesse," she whispered, "I'm not going to make it."

Her words gurgled out, along with blood that bubbled out of the corner of her mouth.

Jesse wiped his shirt sleeve across his eyes. "Masumi," he said. "Remember what I told you…about Jesus. He loves you, Masumi. He died for you. Just…just trust Him…and… you're going to wake up in heaven."

Masumi's eyes closed and her head lolled to one side."

"MASUMI!" Jesse yelled, shaking her.

Masumi's eyes slowly opened. She whispered, "I believe." She then took one last wheezing breath, and once again, her head lolled to one side. She was dead.

"Praise God," Jesse said, and rising slowly, he stood. For several seconds, he just stared at Masumi's inert body. He then wiped his eyes, spun around, and raced toward the front.

Behind him, Masumi's transparent soul slowly rose from her body. Her smiling eyes looked up at Adryel as he reached down, grasped her hand, and said, "Let's go home."

CHAPTER 45

Early Sunday morning.

It was 2:00 a.m. when Ironman, Snake, Bear, and Big Guy arrived back at the Starr Mountain cabin. Their mood matched the roiling clouds and the heavy rain that smacked the rusty tin roof.

Once inside, Ironman fired a glance at Melissa and Woya and her children. He then snapped his head toward Big Guy and said, "GET EM' ON THE BACK PORCH! THE REST OF YOU…ON THE FRONT!"

In the silence that followed, Ironman and the ex-cons gathered on the front porch. Some sat, others stood as Ironman shared what had happened at the prison.

What do we do now?" Smoky asked.

Ironman didn't answer him directly. Instead, he looked at Sanchez and said, "I want you to take the van and get me two things. Snake, Bull, Bear," he said, looking at the three, "go with him."

"It's a little late to go shoppin' don't you think," Bear said. "Check that…a little early."

"I don't give a d___. It's probably better that way. I don't think you're going to find a lot of folks milling around this early on Sunday morning."

"What do you want us to get?" Snake asked.

"A casket and an oxygen tank."

Ten seconds of silence followed until finally, Snake spoke up, "You're kidding…right? I mean, where in the h___ are we going to find that kind of stuff?"

"Where do you think? Use your brain. I suspect you'll find a casket at a funeral home. And I rather imagine you'll find an oxygen tank at one of those medical supply stores."

No one spoke. They just looked at each other then back at Ironman. Ignoring them, he glanced at Slow Beef. Sensing he'd like to go along, he said, "You wanna' go?"

"Yes, boss." Slow Beef was grinning like a child on Christmas morning.

"Okay," he said to the five, "Take off. The sooner you leave, the sooner you'll get back."

On the way out the door, there was a hint of a smile on Ironman's face as he overheard Slow Beef saying, "Hey guys, this is gonna' be fun. It's like…like… a scavenger hunt."

*   *   *

The nearest town to Starr Mountain was Etowah. It was four-point-eight miles away. Ordinarily, it would take about fifteen minutes to get there. Fortunately, the rain had stopped. That would most likely have shortened the time were it not for the fog that engulfed them as they turned right on state highway 39. About twenty minutes later, as they approached a twenty-four hour gas station on their left, the fog lifted. Sanchez pulled the van alongside a pump and shut off the engine.

"Why are we stopping?" Slow Beef asked.

"Well, for one thing," Sanchez said, "I've got to pee. For another, I don't know if there's a funeral home in Etowah or, if there is, where it is. I can't imagine they'd have a medical supply store."

Sanchez slipped out from the steering wheel and before closing the door said, "You guys stay here, unless… you've got to go."

Slow Beef was the only one who got out.

As he entered the brightly lit store, Sanchez quickly noted that, with the exception of the attendant, it was empty. She was behind the counter. He nodded at her as he headed for the facilities, noting that she looked to be at least fifty. Most likely, she was a lot younger. Maybe, no more than late thirties.

A hard scrabble life left its marks on her appearance, etching premature age lines. The missing teeth only added to the deception. Thick makeup and eyeliner only made things worse.

Moments later, Sanchez sauntered up to the counter and asked if there was a funeral home in Etowah. The attendant, who said her name was Misty, said, "Yep. Turn left up ahead, on 411. It's down on your right. You can't miss it. It's a big old house and there's a sign out front. Hastings Funeral Home." She squinted her eyes quizzically and said, "Why are you lookin' for a funeral home at this hour?" It was a little after 3:00 a.m.

"Well," Sanchez said, smiling, "you never know when you might need one." He turned to leave then remembered they needed to find an oxygen tank. "I don't suppose you have a medical supply store in Etowah."

"You're in luck. Hastings has medical supplies, you know—walkers, canes, crutches, and I reckon, oxygen tanks."

"Great. Thanks." To Slow Beef, who had returned from the restroom and was milling between the counter aisles, he said, "Time to go, Bud."

Back in the van, Sanchez followed Misty's directions. He turned left on 411.

A block away, he passed a police car. It was on the left, sitting in the empty parking lot of some tourist gift shop.

"You see that?" Bear said.

"Yeah," Sanchez said as he eased the van passed the squad car. Fortunately, it disappeared from their view as the road curved to the right. Up ahead, about two blocks away, squatted the Hastings Funeral Home. It looked to be a newly remodeled, three story house that had been converted. It had to be at least sixty years old. Maybe older.

Sanchez pulled the van onto the dark parking lot beside the funeral home and shut off the headlights. Just then, a light popped on in the third floor window.

CHAPTER 46

"You see that?" Snake said as he craned his head upward and peered at the lighted window.

"Yeah. I'm afraid so."

"What are we going to do?"

"Sit tight."

Soon, the light from the third floor window blinked off.

Thirty seconds later, the police car they had passed moments ago slowly edged toward the Hastings Funeral Home. Its lights were flashing, sending piercing shards of blue that bounced off the funeral home and the parking lot.

When the squad car reached Hastings, it slowed. Then—it stopped in the middle of the road. Its red brake lights lit up. At the same time, a spot light shot from the squad car and began to prowl the building, and—the parking lot.

Forty-five seconds later, the spotlight and the car's blue lights blinked off and the squad car moved on.

"What now?" Bear said. He was unconsciously whispering.

"We wait to make sure whoever is upstairs is asleep

Five minutes later, Sanchez said, "Let's go." He slid out and gently closed the door. The others did the same.

They followed Sanchez to a side door. He realized it would most likely be locked, but tried it anyway. It was.

"Walk around. Try the windows and see if they might have left one open. If not, we're going to have to break in, and…that's going to make some noise."

While Sanchez remained at the side door, the other four fanned out. They surrounded the building in search of an open window. A few minutes later, they returned. They were all locked.

With no other option, Sanchez slipped back to the van. He opened the rear lift gate and took out the tire tool from its compartment. He returned to the side door and gave the window pane nearest the inside door knob, a sharp whap. It was followed by a loud cracking sound as the glass shattered and tinkled to the ground. Fearing the sound might have awakened whoever was living on the third floor, Sanchez immediately backed away from the door and slipped into a shadow. His eyes snapped up to the third flow window. He held his breath.

Ten seconds.

Twenty.

When the light didn't pop on, he took his first breath. He then reached in through the window pane, found the lock, and twisted it. Soon, they were in a long hallway with doors on both sides. Sanchez opened the first door on the left and was surprised to see caskets. Lots of caskets. They could just make them out by the light that filtered in through the side windows.

"Which one?" Bull asked.

"The lightest."

Moments later, he stepped up beside one that appeared it might be lighter than the others. Without saying a thing, Sanchez pointed to the double outside door which was obviously how they got the large caskets inside. "Open it," Sanchez said to Slow Beef. He and the others then hoisted the casket. And with Sanchez in the lead, his back to the now open door, they walked the casket to the van and slid it inside.

"Now," he said, "let's see if we can find an oxygen tank."

About four minutes after returning to the hallway, they discovered a room with all sorts of medical supplies, including, a couple oxygen tanks. They picked up one and took it back to the van.

"Let's get out of here," Sanchez said.

Fortunately, as they turned left on the main road, there was no sign of the police car. Twenty-five minutes later, they were back at the cabin, unloading the casket and the oxygen tank. It was ten till 5:00.

CHAPTER 47

Both Woya and Melissa were fast asleep. Awakened by the slamming of the van's door, Woya awoke. She got up from the chair in which she had been sleeping, slipped up to the window, and peeked out. *I don't believe it!*

Woya stepped beside Melissa and shook her awake.

"What is it?"

"You're not going to believe it," she said as Melissa joined her at the window in time to see the casket disappear around the side of the cabin.

"What in the world are they doing with a casket?" Melissa asked.

"Beats me, unless…unless it's for Abby. But…that doesn't make sense. Her body is back at the other cabin."

It wasn't until the following evening that they discovered why Ironman had brought a casket to the cabin.

* * *

Monday evening.

It was 8:40 when Ironman appeared before Melissa, Woya and her children and said, "Follow me."

Reluctantly, they did as they were told. Walking behind Ironman, they stepped onto the front porch and down the steps. They walked to the side of the cabin and the outside door to the root cellar. It was open.

Aided by Ironman's flashlight, they descended the steps and walked through the open door below. That's when they saw the casket. It was sitting on saw horses in the center of the dirt floor. The lid was open.

"What's with the casket?" Melissa asked.

When he explained what he was going to do, tears welled up in Woya's eyes. She screamed, "YOU CAN'T DO THAT!"

"Watch me."

Woya looked on wide-eyed and threw her hands to her mouth. Every muscle in her body became taut as Ironman picked up Nathan and injected something into his body. He yelped in pain and cried, "MOMMY." But, seconds later—he was fast asleep.

Ironman laid Nathan's comatose body in the casket. He adjusted a camera lens so it was focused on him. He then closed the lid, turned a knob releasing oxygen into the casket, and locked it. And pulling his cell phone from his pocket, he placed a phone call.

* * *

Expecting to hear from Ironman—Billy, Jesse, and agents Harrelson and McGill sat around the dining table, drinking coffee. Also present were Todd Masterson and one other TBI agent.

Before them was a phone, hooked up to a recording device and a laptop. It was nearly 9:00 p.m. They were beginning to think that Ironman wouldn't call, and were relieved when the phone rang.

Masterson immediately turned on the recorder and nodded at Billy, who picked up the phone.

"This is Billy."

"Good for you. Now listen. We're going to make this exchange once and for all. This is your last chance. You have exactly five hours to cooperate or…"

To increase the tension and drive his point home, Ironman momentarily fell silent.

"…Or what?"

Ironman gave Billy a URL. "Type that into your laptop and you'll see."

Billy gave the URL to Masterson and they all gathered around the computer. Several seconds passed, then Billy saw what no parent should ever have to see.

"OH MY GOD…WHAT HAVE YOU DONE?" Billy said.

It was Nathan. He was lying on a bed of silk in what appeared to be—a casket?

"Allow me to explain what you're seeing. This is your son, Nathan. He's not dead, if that's what you're thinking. But…he is lying in a sealed, air tight casket…"

Billy pushed his chair back from the table. He closed his eyes and looked pleadingly toward heaven. He drew a deep breath and then let his eyes fall back to his son.

"WHAT ARE YOU DOING TO MY SON?"

"Well, fortunately, he doesn't know where he is or what's going on. For you see, believe it or not, I am a compassionate man. I have a terrible case of claustrophobia. When they threw me in solitary confinement, I thought I'd go crazy. Some say I did.

"So, I didn't want your little boy to feel what I felt. So I gave him a shot…"

"A SHOT OF WHAT…?"

"Don't worry about it. Just know this, he'll be fast asleep for five hours. Or let's say, until 2:00 a.m. But after that, he'll wake up, thinking he's buried alive. In a sense he will be, only…he'll be above ground.

"Now, we're pumping oxygen into the casket. It should last another hour after that—until 3:00. So here's the picture, I'm going to give you plenty of time to think about it. I'll call you at about 12:30 and tell you how and where you can get your families back…alive. That is, if… you and Jesse come alone. No cops this time.

"Let me explain that for you, Chief, after I call you, you'll have an hour and a half before your son wakes up and finds himself, as it were…buried alive. Plenty of time. But know this, if you're not here by then, he'll just have to deal with that for another hour until the oxygen runs out. Then…it's…lights out for sure. So… think about it, big guy. I'll call you in three and a half hours. See ya.'"

Ironman hung up.

CHAPTER 48

Unaccustomed to showing emotion, Billy internalized what he had just heard. His face flushed and his eyes glazed. Then to the agents who had gathered in Jesse's cabin, he said, "Give us a minute," and nodding for Jesse to follow him, he entered the bedroom. They both knelt and prayed. *"Lord,"* Billy said, *"we don't know what to do. Please, help us. And please put a wall of protection around Nathan, and our families. I…"* Not knowing what else to say, he said, *"Please."*

Jesse added an *"Amen."*

When they returned to the living room, Harrelson said, "Billy, I know Ironman said you had to go in alone, but you know if you do that, not only are you dead, your families are dead. They've already killed the Cartwrights. They're not going to spare your families. But…I've got an idea."

"What is it?"

"We have access to a FBI drone. It's at the Air National Guard facility at McGhee Tyson. It has thermal imaging capability. I suggest we fly it over Starr Mountain and hopefully, pick up where your families are being held. Once we know, we can send our FBI SWAT team to catch them by surprise. It's a long shot, but…it's a shot."

"Is there enough time?" Jesse asked. "Ironman said he'd call at 12:30 and tells us where our families are. If the deadline is 2:00 a.m., that leaves only an hour and a half."

"Let him call. Billy will tell him that both of you are going to do as he says. He said he drugged Nathan, putting him to sleep for five hours. Let's assume he did that near the time he called, or around 9:00. If by using the drone, we can discover the location by, say…11:00, we should be able to get to McGhee Tyson by 11:30 and leave shortly after. Ironman may think we have only an hour and a half, but we'll actually have two and a half hours to get the SWAT team there and catch them by surprise."

When neither Billy nor Jesse said anything, Harrelson continued, "We've already planned for this possibility. The drone is gassed up. The drone pilot is on standby. So is the SWAT team. All I have to do is place a couple calls. What do you say? You in?"

Billy fired a glance at Jesse. "What do you think?"

"Let's do it!"

"McGill, call Rogers at Air National Guard. Let's get the bird in the air over Starr Mountain. And tell him to send the image to our laptop as soon as he finds the cabin."

Harrelson then called Colonel Aaron Phillips who headed up the SWAT team.

*   *   *

11:10 p.m.

Harrelson's cell phone rang. He snatched it up. It was the drone pilot, Captain Clark. "I think we've found the cabin. I'm sending the image back to you. Let me know when you've got it."

Agents Harrelson and McGill, Billy and Jesse and the two TBI agents gathered around the laptop.

"Can you see it?" Captain Clark said.

"Got it."

On a dark background, the image of a cabin appeared. As the drone circled it, it was clear that there were two doors, one leading to a front porch and another to the back. On the north side of the cabin, there was a door that lay flat on the ground. Like in so many old cabins, it most likely led to an underground tornado and root cellar.

They could see the white image of a man exiting from what appeared to be an outhouse, and there were a couple images of men sitting on the front porch.

"That's great, Captain. What's the GPS?"

Upon receiving it, Harrelson picked up his cell phone to call Colonel Philips.

Seconds later, the Colonel answered. "It's me. Harrelson. Our drone has located the cabin. I'll send you the image. How soon can we take off?"

"Depends on how soon you guys can get here. Can you make it by 11:45?"

"Sure!"

"Then, we can be in the air by 12:00 a.m."

"You know, as I explained, the boy is going to wake up in that casket at 2:00 a.m. That means we only have two hours to get to the cabin and rescue the boy. Can we do that in that time frame?"

There was a pause on the line, after which, the Colonel said, "I…hope so."

CHAPTER 49

Midnight.

To accommodate the SWAT team, the FBI chose to use the larger Sikorsky Black Hawk helicopter. Aboard the chopper were the pilot, Lieutenant Patrick Cooper, Colonel Phillips, Agents Harrelson and McGill, and eight other FBI SWAT team members. After much cajoling, Billy and Jesse were permitted to accompany the SWAT team.

As promised, Ironman had called Billy at 12:30, totally unaware that he, Jesse, and the SWAT team not only knew the location—they were a half hour into their flight.

As the Sikorsky sliced through the air at its top speed of 183 miles per hour,

Billy had feared Ironman would hear the rhythmic "wop-wop" sound of the chopper. If he did, he didn't say anything.

Meanwhile, Colonel Phillips asked the SWAT team to gather around. They all stared at the thermal image of the cabin on the Colonel's laptop.

"Once we're at the cabin, Bud, you and Jake will be with me. We'll take the outside door that leads to the underground root cellar. Brit, you, Gavin and DeMarco take the back door. And Mario, I want you, Brian and Scott to take the front door.

"Lieutenant Cooper is going to land the chopper about a mile from our destination. We don't want to alert our target. Once we get to the cabin, take your positions. If you run into anyone, say…on the porch, quietly, do whatever you have to do to silence them. Then wait till you hear me yell. Got it?"

They all nodded. "Any questions?"

There were none.

*   *   *

It was 1:15 when Cooper found a clearing and landed the Sikorsky. "Okay, listen up everybody," Colonel Phillips said. "We're going the rest the way on foot. Looks like it's about a mile. I'll lead the way." To Harrelson, Billy, and Jesse, he said, "You guys keep a good distance from the cabin when we get there."

The Colonel glanced at his watch and said, "We've got forty-five minutes to get to the cabin, neutralize Ironman and the ex-cons, and find and get Billy's son out of that casket before he wakes up.

"OKAY…LET'S GO!"

Colonel Phillips leaped out of the chopper and began running in the direction of the cabin. The eight SWAT team members were close behind, followed by Harrelson, Billy, and Jesse.

For the next thirty minutes, they dodged trees and branches, and stepped over and around downed limbs as they raced toward the cabin. Above, treetops swayed and shook under gusty winds. Periodically, patches of moonlight filtered through the dark clouds that scudded across the moon.

It was 1:45 when they reached the cabin, just fifteen minutes before Nathan would awaken. Silently, the SWAT team crept to their positions and waited for the Colonel's signal.

CHAPTER 50

"GO, GO, GO!"

Simultaneously, Brit, Gavin and DeMarco smashed in the back door and rushed inside, rifles and flashlights leading the way while Mario, Brian and Scott burst through the front door, yelling, "FBI…FBI…FBI. STAY STILL. DON'T MOVE!"

In total confusion, the ex-cons awoke. One stepped through a bedroom door brandishing a Keltec 38. He fired off a quick shot. It lit the area around him. The sound echoed through the living quarters and zipped close to DeMarco. He quickly returned fire. The bullet struck whoever it was. It raised him off the floor and smacked his now inert body against the door frame.

By the time the first shot was fired, Colonel Phillips had already grasped the handle of the outside cellar door and flung it open. With Bud and Jake close behind, he charged down the concrete steps. He quickly hoisted a plank that rested on side brackets, securing the door, and tossed it aside. He then yanked open the bottom door to the cellar and yelled, "FBI. DON'T ANYONE MOVE!"

At first, even with his flashlight probing the cellar's interior, he was unable to make out any details except for—

The casket.

It sat on two saw horses in the middle of the cellar. A solitary candle was stuck to its top in a puddle of wax. Its flame danced, sending out flickering, staccato patches of light. Anyone with a heightened sense of imagination might swear that the cellar was alive. Breathing.

And then—he saw them. Woya, Chloe, and Melissa. They were huddled in a corner. A patch of candlelight swept over them, then disappeared.

Colonel Phillips thrust his flashlight in their direction. "Mrs. Whitecloud? Mrs. Striker?"

He rushed over to them. "It's okay. It's okay! We're FBI! You're safe!"

Just then—

The Colonel sensed movement. It was coming from his right. *Was someone else in the cellar?*

Phillips quickly thrust a shaft of light in the direction of where he had sensed a presence. Its light passed through Adryel who was standing in the far corner, his head nearly touching the eight-foot ceiling.

Woya jumped up and said, "MY BOY. HE'S...HE'S IN THE CASKET!"

Phillips cast a quick glance at his watch. It was 1:55 a.m. Just five minutes before the boy would awaken.

"I know, ma'am. We're going to get him out."

As he said that, Bud had already stepped beside the casket and was attempting to lift the lid, but—it wouldn't budge.

219

"It's locked," Jake said.

His uncle was a funeral director and he knew that before burial, caskets were cranked shut to make them air tight. Knowing that a key would be inserted in a hole on the side to crank it open or shut, he quickly slipped past Bud. He ran his hand where the crank should be, but— it wasn't there. Instead, a screw-in cap blocked the hole. That gave rise to a thought he had no intention of verbalizing. *Whoever put the boy in the casket had no intention of him getting out alive.*

Jake nonetheless said, "LOOK FOR A KEY!"

It was 1:56 a.m.

"WHAT'S IT LOOK LIKE?" yelled Colonel Phillips.

"It's above five inches long," Jake said as he, Bud, and Jake hurriedly rummaged and fumbled through sagging wooden shelves. It's "L" shaped."

1:58 a.m.

"HURRY!" Woya screamed.

Suddenly, there was swift movement coming from the far corner of the cellar. It was Adryel. Had they been able to see him, it would seem as if he had apparated from the corner to the casket. The truth is, he had. He towered over it. And reaching his huge hands over the top, he felt for the slit that separated the lid from the base and—gave it a yank.

1:58:30

There was a loud, metallic ripping and popping sound as the lock snapped loose and the casket top flew open.

Momentarily, everyone froze. Their eyes locked on the now open casket lid that had somehow miraculously popped open.

1:59 a.m.

Bud and Jake, who were now standing before the open casket, quickly looked inside. Bud fired a glance in Woya's direction. "He's breathing ma'am," he said. "He's going to be okay." He then reached in, slid his arms under the boy, gently lifted him from the casket, and carried him to his mother.

CHAPTER 51

2:00 a.m.

As Woya sat and rocked Nathan—Colonel Phillips, Bud, and Jake stood silently. Melissa was at Woya's side, her arm around her shoulder. Chloe sat at her mother's feet.

Woya looked up at Melissa then back to the Colonel. "Are our husbands here?"

"Yes, ma'am. They're outside. I'll go get them."

"NO…wait," Melissa said. "My husband, Jesse… doesn't know about Abigail."

"I don't understand."

"Abby…Abigail is our only daughter. She was ten…"

"Was?"

"She tried to run away and get help, but…but she has, she *had* a terrible case of asthma and…and…she didn't make it. She died."

"Oh…I'm so sorry, ma'am."

"I…I don't think I could tell him. Please, will you do it?" Tears began to trickle down Melissa's cheeks.

"Of course…of course."

Colonel Phillips turned, slowly walked up the concrete steps and stood before Jesse and Billy.

"Are they okay?" Jesse asked.

"Yeah. But…I've got to share something with you, Jesse."

A moment of silence followed as the Colonel tried to think of how best to tell Jesse what had happened to his daughter.

"Jesse, it's about Abigail."

"If you're going to tell me that…she's dead, I already know."

"You do? Melissa thought you didn't."

"There's no way she could have known that I do. Knoxville's FBI bureau chief, Billy, and I flew down to the cabin where she, Abby, and Billy's family were being held. We found Abby's body."

"Okay…okay. Well, just so you know that Melissa doesn't know…that *you* know."

Colonel Phillips then said to Billy and Jesse, "You guys ready to see your families?"

At that, the Colonel led Billy and Jesse toward the steps that descended to the root cellar.

* * *

While Billy and Jesse headed for the root cellar, Harrelson placed a call to the Knoxville Police and the TBI. He informed them on what had taken place and asked them to pick up Ironman and his gang and take them to the county jail. While he was still on the phone, Billy crossed the threshold to the root cellar. Jesse was close behind.

When Billy ducked inside, Woya burst into tears and stood with Nathan in her arms. Billy hurried to her side. With one arm around Chloe, he hugged his wife with the other. As he did, Nathan began to awaken. "Daddy…" he said.

Jesse stepped within three feet of Melissa. They stood, staring at each other, tears flowing. "It's okay, baby," Jesse said as he walked up to her. He put his hands on either side of her face, and kissed her on the forehead, the cheeks, and the lips. "I love you so much!"

A few moments later, Melissa pulled back from Jesse and said, "Jesse, about Abby…"

Melissa choked up and couldn't finish. "Her body…."

Knowing what Melissa was going to say, Jesse interrupted her. He shared that he had been to the cabin where they had been held and that he had recovered Abby's body. "We took her to Anderson Funeral Home. In Sevierville. So… when we get back, we can give her a proper burial."

"Praise God!" Melissa said, once again blinking away tears of relief.

"Meanwhile, let's just keep our focus on the truth that Abby's in heaven with Jesus!"

With Chloe at her side, Woya set Nathan on the dirt floor, then she and Billy reached out their arms to Jesse and Melissa. As they stood, arms around each other and their hands on the kids shoulders, Billy said, "May the circle be unbroken."

And they all said, "Amen!"

CHAPTER 52

Five days later.

Saturday.

11:00 a.m.

A "Celebration of Life" funeral service for Abigail was held at 10:00 a.m. at Fellowship Church. An hour later, Jesse, Melissa, Billy, Woya and their children met at the Headrick Chapel for a brief private graveside service.

Located on a small hillside in Wears Valley, Headrick Chapel—with its subtle Gothic Revival influences, small open belfry and steeply pitched roof—has a coveted place on the "National Register of Historic Places." Its breathtaking view of the Smoky Mountains is but an added plus that has drawn hundreds to paint and photograph the historic Chapel.

Over one hundred years old, the tiny cemetery beside the chapel is dotted with moss and mildew darkened tombstones dating to the Civil War. The oldest marks the spot of a Revolutionary War Fifer.

Following the death of Jenny, Jesse was surprised to have been able to secure two remaining plots on the slope of Headrick's Hill. Resting before a black marble headstone, lay the body of Jenny Striker. On the adjacent plot, a smaller, matching, black marble tombstone marked Abby's resting place. It read ABIGAIL STRIKER, followed by the years of her brief time on earth. Beneath that were the words, "At Home With Jesus."

Given the circumstances surrounding her death, Abigail had been cremated and was soon after, buried. Now, Pastor Carter stood facing the tombstone. Billy, Woya, Chloe, and Nathan stood to his left, Jesse and Melissa to his right. Adryel stood unseen not more than ten feet away.

Looking at the Strikers, Pastor Carter said *"Jesse, Melissa,"* and to the Whiteclouds, *"Billy, Woya,"* then their children, *"Chloe and Nathan—we have gathered to remember the heroic life of Abigail.*

"But first, let us pray: 'Father in heaven, we grieve because Abigail is no longer with us here on earth. But we rejoice for we know that through her faith in Jesus Christ, she is with You. And that…is far better. And the short life she lived was truly…heroic. Comfort, I pray, Jesse and Melissa, Billy, Woya and their children, as only You can. We ask it in Jesus blessed name…amen!'

"In that brief prayer, I spoke of Abigail's short life as having been heroic. And…it truly was. Our Lord Jesus once said, 'Greater love has no one than this: to lay down one's life for one's friends.'

"The supreme example of that is the life of Jesus. As Scripture says, 'He came not to be served, but to serve, and give His life as a ransom for many.' I submit to you, that Abigail did something similar. Hoping to save her mother,

Woya, Chloe, and Nathan, she snuck out of the cabin in which they were all being held. She gave no thought to her asthmatic condition; her only thought was to save those she loved. She died in the process. That's…heroic.

"You know, there are rewards in heaven beyond our salvation. We don't know what they are, but know this, for her faith and for her act of love as she attempted to save those she loves…I have no doubt she will be rewarded by our heavenly Father."

Pastor Carter paused. He looked at Jesse and Melissa, and then down at the spot where Abigail's ashes had been buried, and said, *"And now, forasmuch as it has pleased Almighty God, in His wise providence, to take out of this world the soul of Abigail Striker, we commit her body to the ground—earth to earth, ashes to ashes, dust to dust—in the sure hope of the resurrection to eternal life.*

"May God the Father, who has created this body, may God the Son who by His blood has redeemed this body together with the soul, and may God the Holy Spirit who has sanctified this body to be His temple—keep these remains until the day of the resurrection of all flesh. We ask it in Jesus name…amen!"

CHAPTER 53

Four months later

Jesse's mind flitted back to twelve years ago when he had first visited Ironman at Georgia State Prison. Everything was as he remembered. Except, this time, Ironman was not in prison for life; he was on death row.

Once again, Jesse stepped into the long, narrow, rectangular room. And once again he flinched at the sound of the iron door as it clanked shut behind him.

To Jesse's left, were the same battleship gray cinderblocks. To his right, running the full length of the hallway, were numerous cubicles that separated the corridor he was in from an identical one on the other side.

On both sides of each cubicle, separated by thick Plexiglas, was a metal chair. For a modicum of privacy, on either side of the Plexiglas was a floor-to-ceiling, perpendicular partition.

The guard who had led Jesse into the visiting corridor pointed to a chair. Jesse took a deep breath and sat. A minute later, another guard led Ironman to the other side of the Plexiglas. Jesse picked up the wall phone. Ironman did the same.

"We meet again," Jesse said.

Ironman said nothing.

After an intense period of silence, Jesse said, "We both know that it's just a matter of time before they take your life. It'll be awhile. You can have all your appeals, but I think you know that you're not getting out of here… alive."

Ironman showed no emotion. He just glared at Jesse.

"I wanted to speak to you one last time. Not only did you kill my wife, Jenny, twelve years ago, you are the cause of my daughter Abigail dying.

"I'd like to say, as I did twelve years ago, that I forgive you, but…that would be a lie. I want to, but…I'm not there yet. I'm working on it. Hopefully…I'll get there one day. But, I want you to know something, something I shared with you twelve years ago.

"I want you to know that even if I'm never able to forgive you…God is. In spite of all you have done, He still loves you. He still wants to forgive you, and…He will… if you let Him."

A moment of silence followed as Jesse and Ironman stared at one another.

"You know, you're going to be executed. You can't change that. It's called consequences. But listen to me. Everyone sins. Everyone is going to die. And everyone is going to live forever. Somewhere. Either in heaven or hell. And that's true whether you believe it or not.

"And…in spite of all you've done, like I said, God will forgive you if you trust in Jesus Christ. He died to earn you a place in heaven. If you just believe that, and trust

229

in Him, when you draw your last breath, you will wake up there."

For Jesse, this was deja vu to the max. Twelve years ago, he had shared the same message to Ironman. Obviously, it didn't take. Would it this time?

Jesse stared at him for ten seconds, then said, "That's all I've got to say." He placed the phone on the wall mount and stood.

Ironman looked upward. His eyes glistened as he stared at Jesse. He made no effort to hide it. Instead, he cleared his throat and spoke. "I…I…"

Jesse again lifted the phone off its cradle to hear what Ironman was trying to say. But try as he did, the words wouldn't come out. Ironman squeezed his eyes tightly shut and just…shook his head. His voice broke as he said, "I'd like to believe, but…"

Ironman didn't finish the sentence. He just stood quickly, so quickly, the chair behind him clattered to the floor. And spinning around, he yelled, "GUARD!"

CHAPTER 54

One year later.

"There's a letter for you," Melissa said as she walked up the concrete drive and onto the steps of the front porch. Jesse was sitting on one of the two matching rocking chairs. Melissa joined him on the nearby swing.

"Who's it from?"

Melissa turned the letter over and said, "It says GEORGIA DEPARTMENT OF CORRECTIONS." She handed the letter to Jesse. He opened it and read it to himself. They sat in silence for a full thirty seconds.

"What does it say?"

Jesse slowly turned his gaze toward Melissa. "It's about Ironman. They're going to execute him a couple months from now. In June. On the fifteenth. It's an invitation for you and me to witness it."

Once again, they sat in silence. Melissa broke it. "Do you want to go?"

Jesse looked up and over at Melissa, "You?"

"The last thing I want to see is a man being administered a lethal injection."

Seconds later, Jesse said, "Maybe it would give us some closure."

Over the ensuing month, after much prayer, Jesse and Melissa decided to attend the execution of Beau Haggart, alias Ironman. Billy and Woya had also received an invitation, but declined.

It was a rainy Saturday afternoon in June, a little past 1:15, when Jesse and Melissa pulled up to the razor wire fence that surrounded Georgia State Prison. Northwest winds sent dust devils spiraling wildly as they drove up to and stopped in front of the guard gate.

Thirty minutes later, at precisely 1:45 p.m., Jesse and Melissa took seats before a mostly glass, institutionally white, octagonal structure. It was about twenty-five feet in diameter. Approximately thirty others—victims, friends, family, and curiosity seekers had also come to witness the execution of Beau Haggart.

He lay on his back, strapped to a permanent gurney with an IV in each arm. At a minute before 2:00, a guard opened the inside curtains. Standing beside Beau Haggart, he said, "Do you have any last words?"

With much difficulty, Haggart lifted his head off the gurney. He was clearly squinting through the glare of the interior lighting, trying to see who had come. And then his eyes locked on Melissa, and then Jesse.

He said, "I do." Then, with a smile of contentment on his face, he directed four words to Jesse and Melissa. He said, "I believe in Jesus."

Beau Haggart then lowered his head. He was administered three drugs: sodium thiopental to induce unconsciousness, pancuronium bromide to cause muscle paralysis and respiratory arrest, and lastly, potassium chloride to stop his heart.

Proving that God is a God of love, willing, even eager to forgive any and all who will trust in the merits of His Son Jesus Christ, seven minutes later—Beau Haggart woke up in heaven.

*   *   *

The drive from Reidsville, Georgia to their Wears Valley, Tennessee home took nearly three hours. Neither Jesse nor Melissa could get over the fact that Ironman had actually been brought to faith in Jesus. For those three hours, the joy they felt dispelled the grief they had over the death of Abigail.

At 5:35, they pulled up the drive to their cabin. They made a pot of coffee and sat in silence on the back porch. And then—something happened. Something remarkable.

Jesse was the first to sense it. It was the smell of perfume. Jenny's perfume.

"Do you smell that?" Jesse stared at Melissa.

Melissa cast him a wide-eyed smile and nodded.

That's when both of them saw Jenny's angel. She was standing to their right, near the steps of the back porch. Both Jesse and Melissa were staring right through her. They could see the trees on the other side of the driveway.

Jenny's angel wore a big smile, as she looked first at Jesse and Melissa and then down to her right. Her arm was lovingly nestled around the shoulder of…

"Abigail?" Jesse said.

It was…Abby's angel. She too was smiling, and then—both she and Jenny gradually faded away.

EPILOGUE

"Well, that's the story of Jesse Striker, his wife Melissa and their daughter Abigail…and the story of Billy Whitecloud, Woya, and their children, Chloe and Nathan. It's a story about the horrendous things they had experienced. As the angel called to watch over them, I was able to help them through some difficult times, but… not all. And I know, some of you are wondering why that is? It's that age old question that haunts all of you. 'Why do bad things happen to good people?' Let me answer that in this way.

"First, you must realize…there are no good people, per say. Sure, some folks are better than others, but none are good in the sense of being good enough to deserve being in God's heaven. That would take perfection. And obviously, no human can achieve that.

"Do you not recall what Jesus said about the goodness of man? It's in your Bibles. A man came up to our Lord and said, '*Good teacher, what must I do to inherit eternal life?*' Jesus didn't answer his question at first. Instead, He said, '*Why do you call me good? No one is good—except God alone.*'

"Now, Jesus *is* God. And being God—He, the Father and the Spirit—our Triune God—is good. Were I to

paraphrase what our Lord said, it might sound like this…
'given I have told you that only God is good, do you recognize that I, Jesus…am God.' But more to my point, no
one…no ordinary human being…is good.

"Secondly, when our Father finished creating the
world, He said, 'it is good.' But from then on things took a
turn for the worse. From that day forward, man has been
in charge of God's good creation. And everything bad you
now find on earth is *man's* doing…not God's.

"It was the man Cain who killed Able, not God. It
was man who flew planes into the Twin Towers killing
over 3,000 men, women, and children, not God. It is man,
radical Islamists who behead and crucify…even little
children. Man! Not God!

"'Yes,' someone will say, 'but He could stop the bad
things.' That's true. He could. But here's the problem. God
has given man a free will, and given man's fallen nature,
more times than not, he uses it in a bad way.

"The bottom line is this; it is a mistake to blame
God for what man does. You live in a world of sin, and
there's no way to avoid being affected by it…in one way
or another. And given your free will, and that of others,
neither I nor any angel is capable of stopping *all* the bad
things that man brings upon himself, and others.

"But it would be good to remember that whenever
possible, your guardian angel can and will, in many circumstances, protect you. It would also be good to remember that for those of you who trust in Christ, no matter

how bad something may seem, or for that matter, may be—God will bring you through it, and bring something good out of it.

"Sound impossible? Remember God's Son, Jesus Christ. He was brutalized and crucified. And yet, He is now alive and will be the ruler of the new earth. And He forgives and promises eternal life to all who trust in Him. How's that for something good coming out of something …bad?

"Lastly, I close with this admonition: trust in Jesus. For it was He who left heaven and came to the earth to live a perfect life for you, fulfilling heaven's entrance requirement of perfection on your behalf. And it was He who died on a cross to pay the penalty for your sins. All who believe that, and trust in Him, receive forgiveness and the promise of eternal life.

"So, when it comes to the remainder of your brief life on earth, nothing… absolutely nothing is more import-ant than… trusting in Jesus." –Adryel.